Candy Cane

'This Christmas, the naughty list is final...'

Katye Tilstone

Candy Cane

Candy Cane

Author Notes:

Season's Greetings to you my reader, I hope you're ready to step into the festive spirit with this newest edition. 'Tis the season for love and laughter however, within these pages the screams drown out the silent night. So, join me on this festive ride only if you're brave enough not to hide. Come on! Be quick! Don't step on the candy sticks! Naughty or Nice we all pay the price. Now go, be nimble and quick before you hear the horn blow and the bells become louder.

Candy Cane

Trigger Warnings:

The ritual in progress and sleigh bells ringing here are a list of some of the warnings within this book, stay safe and lock your doors. Remember he is always watching... If the following is too much for you, turn away now and hopefully you'll be on his good list...

- *Extreme Gore/Bodily Dismemberment*
- *Hemophobia (Blood)*
- *Children Endangerment/Death*
- *Graphic Violence/ Bodily Horror*
- *Cannibalism*
- *Abuse*
- *Sexual Themes*
- *Suspenseful Scenes*
- *Mental Health Illness*
- *Forced Captivity*
- *Torture*

Candy Cane

- *Religious Aspects*
- *Possession*
- *Gaslighting*
- *Alcohol Abuse*
- *Self-Harming*
- *Germophobia/Mysophobia*

If any of the following themes disturb you or make you feel uncomfortable you are advised to stop here, thank you for the constant support and we hope you have a holly jolly Christmas filled with love and laugher, instead of screams of terror. Lock your doors as his jingles come this way, the ancient horn blasting louder. Santa isn't the only one checking his list tonight and it looks like you're on his underlined in red.

Candy Cane

Prologue:

The cold wasn't just a temperature; it was a weight. It settled over the snow crusted clearing like a shroud, crushing the sound out of the late-night woods. The only sound was the brittle crunch of frozen gravel under his worn leather boots.

He didn't hear the carols anymore. The laughter, the frantic consumerism was all drowned out by the deep, insistent drumming of the cloven hoof in his own chest. They called him Santa. They called the other, the true one; the horned shadow. He was the balance. The judge who corrects the cosmic mistake of misplaced kindness.

Tonight's offering was complete, the justice served. The scarlet stain a deep, bruised colour against the blinding white was already beginning to freeze. He worked with

the patient devotion of a priest, his heavy, moth-eaten red coat a purposeful insult over the scene.

Candy Cane

He reached into the damp pocket. The peppermint aroma was sharp and clinical on his tongue as his gloved fingers closed around the familiar shape. He ran a thumb over the razor thin point of the cane; not a festive treat, but a tool of surgical precision. A beautiful mockery.

With the precision of a jeweller, he broke the hooked end clean off, the peppermint snap echoing unnaturally loud in the silence. The broken piece, the deadly point was inserted into the frozen ground right beside his victim.

A signature. A warning. A ritual tribute to the old tales, to the one who punishes when the fool rewards. He smiled, feeling the familiar joyous cruelty of the Krampus take hold.

This Christmas, the reckoning had arrived. And it smelled sickeningly sweet.

Candy Cane

Chapter One:

'Comfort and Joy...'

The cold winters breeze blew through the naked frost-bitten trees as small droplets of white flakes cascaded to the ground. It was that time again as the aroma of cinnamon and gingerbread wafted through the air, children's laughter echoed as did the grumbles of unhappy parents trying to get their children to behave for the holiday season.

"He's always watching, you better be good or you'll get coal." Parents would shout at misbehaving children, and with the threat of no presents other than a lump of coal, it seemed to settle them; even if only for a moment. Shops were illuminated by fluorescent multi-coloured lights, carol singer's voices rang through the dusted old speakers as the cheerful jolly man himself sat on his velvet chair, welcoming all the innocent children to sit on his lap. His beard was white as winters snow

Candy Cane

as his fat belly hid just barely behind his crimson red coat. His pink, rosy cheeks were flushed from being out in the frozen snow, and thin half framed glasses hung just at the end of his large nose. He was not the real Santa Claus of course, but someone who's years of acting school had landed them a simple 'Mall Santa' job.

"Ho, Ho, Ho!" His trademark laugh, nothing new, nothing out of the ordinary. However, if you looked closer, you'd see parts of his face that didn't quite seem the same; how his eyelids blinked, but his face took on that ghostly pale shade. Thanks to the white wig and fake facial hair, no one noticed the corners of his face starting to peel off, as if it was a fruit that had been left out in the sun for too long. The dried crimson redness of blood had now flaked into the pure white fake hair, and his face seemed to droop on one side more than the other. The sinister smell of decay was hidden behind the overpowering odour of a sickly sweet peppermint, coming from the candy canes that were

Candy Cane

wrapped in translucent paper and tied with a bright red silk bow; holding the sweet treat together within its paper cage.

Looking onto an array of different sized presents that were wrapped in red and green striped paper, with golden velvet bows placed upon the tops of them, it peaked the children's interests; making their minds wonder at the possibility of what was inside them. A brand-new ruby red toy car, or maybe the new 'Britney Doll' that all the young girls wanted this year; in her pink ballet dress, with her brunette hair tied up neatly in a bun, a small plastic tiara stabled to the top of her crown. The possibilities were endless to the children's imaginations of what might be hiding behind the colourful boxes.

Sleigh bells rang signalling for the fat man himself to move, his belly jiggling like a pot of jelly as he stood in his worn-out black winter boots, connecting to the laminated floor. Reaching his fingerless glove behind the

Candy Cane

chair, he retrieved a beat-up sign and placed it up onto the velvet chair. The sign read *'Gone to feed Rudolph, be back in 10 minutes...'*

Children's cries and pleads scorched through the endless line of parents wanting to get that perfect picture of their child, sat on a stranger's lap, classing it as 'childhood memories' whilst their young child is terrified by the stranger man holding them; probably smelling of whisky. The 'elves' would come to try and calm the endless line of screaming children, handing out the intoxicating candy canes. Again, the elves were either theatre student dropouts or poor souls who needed the money; having to walk around in fluorescent green dresses that were made from polyester with low-quality stitching, and they fell apart at the seams. The pointed hats were equipped with a small golden bell that jingled everywhere they went, like dogs on a leash.

Candy Cane

Each step clicked across the laminated floor like walking on ice as the 'Santa Claus' disappeared, slipping inside a darkened room. No one could see into the horrors that he was just about to endure, as the fingerless gloves reached up, gripping the fake white hair and pulling it off swiftly. The jolly face and domineer changed as dried blood flaked off the skinned face, as if they were their own snowflakes. Facing the mirror across from him, William stared at his blood-soaked face, his own features sunken in as his eyes were bloodshot from the countless nights of overworking.

"Not long now, naughty or nice- it'll be your time." His voice deep as he heard the ancient horn blaring in his head, his heart pounding like cloven hoofs against his ribs.

Candy Cane

Chapter Two:

'Deck the halls...'

A month prior to the slaughter, the excitement of the festive holiday was in full swing as the mall started gathering decorations, half a dozen sparkling snowflakes dangling from the ceiling. Lights reflected off the colourful foil strings of tinsel. Blues, greens and reds created a darkened rainbow across the mall floor, whereas the silver beamed lights of joy were almost as if the heavens had opened their gates for a splitting moment. The golden rays of tinsel created a halo as if angels had blessed the ground the shoppers walked upon.

Human sized baubles swung off the ceiling in a variety of colours and shapes, glitter dripping off them and creating a magical experience. There was a combination of snowflakes and tinsel, alongside a large dark pine tree where a star shun brightly upon the top of it; like a

Candy Cane

beckon to the passersby that the wonderful time of the year will soon be here. The line stretched far across the shop floor, full of people who needed the seasonal job as the one and only 'Santa Claus'. Some of the other candidates would inevitably end up as his working staff, the 'elves'. Some people were already showing the characteristics of the jolly man himself, with their white hair or long white beard; some not needing padding for a round belly.

William stood, thinner than most, and his face was dull and emotionless; with dull blue eyes which carried dark black bags under them. His short brown hair was caked in grease and sweat lead down to his unkept beard, where bits of stale breadcrumbs sat from his sandwich earlier. His darkened blue postal office uniform was creased and stained with an unusual substance, and his bodily odour smelt as if he had just bathed with a skunk.

Candy Cane

"William Miller, you're next!" A tall woman shouted through the rowdy crowd of people; her blonde hair tied back into a high ponytail as her large framed black glasses took up the majority of her face. Holding his head down, William gathered the courage and shakily walked toward the woman. Inching closer to her, the light shimmered on the plastic badge that was on the left side of her blazer that said 'Manager.'

Entering the dimly lit office, William noticed the stack of papers on the wooden table. Two green chairs stood in front of him, his breath caught in his throat as the overwhelming aroma of the seasonal vanilla spice, mixed with cinnamon invaded his nose. The sickly-sweet stench caught in the back of his throat, staggering William as he placed his dirty covered hand upon the chairs material to steady himself, and suddenly the door slammed shut behind him.

"I'm sorry I didn't mean to slam the door. I'm the manager here at Gloomhaven's Mall. I'm Susan Jones,

Candy Cane

welcome!" Susan greeted, extending her arm out towards William, her fresh manicure sparkling golden specks on top of the bright red base under the light. Her face was smothered under layers of foundation as her lipstick matched her nails; bright red with small golden specks, smiling showing her pearly white symmetrical teeth.

Lifting his other hand, William wiped the sweat drenched hand on his uniform before placing it into Susan's, grasping it firmly as he smiled with his off-white teeth stained by coffee, blindingly unaware of the piece of lettuce still stuck in between his top two teeth. Nodding briefly as their hands held contact, Susan gestured towards the desk with her spare arm as she slithered away, wiping her sweat infested hand on the chair after grabbing a bottle of hand sanitizer. Squirting it into her hand, she franticly massaged the clinical smelling gloop into her hands. William sunk down slightly embarrassed into the green chair as he looked

Candy Cane

across at the wet slapping noise coming from Susans frantic rubbing with the hand sanitizer.

"So, you've applied to be one of our Santa Clauses. Can you tell me a bit about yourself and why you think we should consider you?" Susan barked as she peered over her glasses towards the germ-infested mess in front of her.

"Well, I'm a hard worked, I've been with the postal office for going on fifteen years now, and I want a chance to make children believe in the spirit of Christmas. I have two of my own. I've studied all the folklore about Santa and the fact his true origin was based on a real person." William grinned. Not many people knew or believed that the origin of the jolly present bringer was based on a real man in the 4th century, a bishop known as St. Nicholas.

"Very good, you know your fokelore however, I'm afraid we have a certain health code that we have to follow. Mr. Miller I'm afraid that your frame and overall

Candy Cane

look is not what we are looking for, within Santa Claus or an elf." Susan snorted as she tilted her head up, now looking down towards William's deflated domineer.

"Hold on, I can fix my hygiene. I am a very hard worker... please I really need this job! Susan please!" William begged as he lunged forward latching onto her hands, that overpowering smell of clinical aroma seeping into his sinuses. Tears prickled the corners of his bloodshot eyes as his grip grew tighter around her hands.

"Mr. Miller, get your disgusting hands off me before I call for security!" Susan squealed like a pig at the sudden assault, clawing frantically at Williams strong grip trying to pray her hands free.

"Susan please! I really need this job for my kids, please!" William begged harder as his fingernails dug into her porcelain skin, drawing a small amount of blood. The darkened redness dripped down her pure innocent skin as she wailed louder.

Candy Cane

Managing to wriggle her left hand out, Susan frantically grabbed the hand sanitizer bottle and squirted it towards William's eyes. He fell back onto the ground pleading for another chance, whilst he screamed about his eyes burning. Susan shouted for security as two large men dressed in black burst through the door, each holding onto William's arms hosting him up as they dragged him out.

"You'll regret this! Fuck you Susan Jones!" William's voice echoed through the busy crowd as Susan dug into her desk draw, bringing out a brand-new air freshener with the scent 'Cinnamon spice,' spraying it around the dirt invaded room.

Candy Cane

Chapter Three:

'All I want for Christmas is...'

Humiliated wasn't the word that William felt. Something else had snapped that day, his Christmas spirit dissipating like the snow did once the weather warmed up. Walking through the busy town streets that were filled with parents rushing to get their children's Christmas list wants, William took a sharp left turn, down a narrow path . That's when he spotted it; a small old Victorian like shop wedged between two broken shops. The outside looked as if the paint was wearing off, but the vibrant colours of green and red still caught his eyes as above the shop itself, written in chipped wood was 'Spielzeugladen.'

"What the fuck is this?" He mumbled still wiping the hand sanitiser out of his teary eyes that felt as if they would explode at any given minute.

Candy Cane

Walking closer to the shop, his curiosity getting the better of him, William peered inside the frosted window; seeing wooden dolls and cars. Candy Canes draped across the counter as the shop itself seemed like a child's wonderland full of candy, toys and festive joy that now made him feel disgusted.

"Fuck this holiday, I'm sick of seeing this shit everywhere. I try to be a good father, a good husband, but they hate me. I work **72** hours a week to deliver their fucking presents in time for Christmas and not a single thank you. Christmas is dead to me." William spat on the frosted window as he turned to walk away, until something caught his eye, glimmering by the front door, and that was when he heard it for the first time.

A bell, as clear as day, captivating him into some sort of trance; his body moving towards the cracked wooden door. He placed his hand upon the silver ice cold handle, pushing it gently as the door swung open with ease; letting the cold winters breeze drift in. Peering

Candy Cane

around the seemingly empty toy shop, wooden toys littered the shelves from brightly coloured boats, to cars and dolls. There were puppets made of wood with cloth clothing dangling from their thin strings, being pushed gently by the sudden breeze.

A counter sat in the middle of the childhood toys, draped in wrapping paper, a dark green with the deepest of red stripes as mistletoe pictures cascaded in every corner. Golden long scissors shimmered in the dim light as did the different variety of velvet ribbons ranging from, gold, silver, blue and red. Gift tags were stacked besides them showing an array of characters from Reindeer, Elves, Gingerbread men, Snow men, and also Mr Claus & Mrs Claus; sat in his large, bright red sleigh and surrounded by presents.

To the far left sat a dusted, old blue velvet armchair. The shelves behind were encased in a decade's worth of dust and cobwebs, as the books spines sat untouched. Each one were of the folklore stories of old

Candy Cane

St. Nick, from Rudolph helping save Christmas to the magical snowman that came alive at just the touch of an old hat. Holiday spirits visiting an elderly man who lost his seasonal spirit to help him regain it, from Jack Frost to the witch 'Grýla' who would adventure down from her icy mountains, just to use the holiday to steal naughty children to eat for her Christmas feast. Even the rarest of folklores such as 'The Yule Cat', a massive ferocious creature like feline that would lurk in the icy countryside and would prey on those who did not receive new clothing during the Christmas season.

William inched closer to the bookcase, his curiosity growing fonder as he reached towards the only book out of its dusted time capsule. Rested on the armchairs pillow sat the book, wrapped in a leather-bound brown cover with golden corners. The title written in bold red cursive *'Krampen'* alongside the illustration of a golden bell and a ram horn placed behind it, drawn in golden ink. A golden scuffed buckled held it shut, and whilst shaking like an addict without his fix, William bent down

Candy Cane

towards the book and grasped it with his still blood and dirt covered hands.

"Holy shit, is this..." William whispered holding the cold leather book in his still shaking hands, "Is this the legend of Krampus?" His breath was icy from the cold breeze as the hair on the back of his neck stood up. As a chill ran down his spine, he felt as if he was being watched.

"Excuse me sir?" A woman's frail voice spoke behind him, almost making his drop the ancient book.

"Ah! Fuck! Sorry you scared me!" William shouted back as his grip grew tighter on the leather-bound book, not wanting to cause it any damage.

"Zhat is my book, how can I helpz you today?" She asked again, her German accent slipping out slightly as her wrinkled old face looked up towards the towering man before her.

Candy Cane

Her eyes were sunken into her skull, barely able to make out the colour of them as her frazzled, long grey hair draped over her shoulders and down her back. A red and green knitted blanked hidden under her hair lay across her shoulders and back, while her black silk dress pulled across the floor. Her glasses were perched on the end of her short button nose, attached to a knitted string around her neck. One of her hands, you could see her bones stretching through her frail translucent skin as she clutched it around the knitted blanked, the other stayed hidden to the side of her.

"Oh, yes sorry, I'm William I was just passing by and saw your lovely shop, so I thought I'd come in, and I saw this." He spat quickly gesturing to the book.

Candy Cane

Chapter Four:

'Believe in the magic...'

Her thin lips curved up into a gentle smile. The old woman waved with her hidden arm for William to follow her behind the counter, which was cluttered with wrapping paper. Unsure why and riddled with curiosity, William followed.

"Zhis was ma family's shop, I has been wzorking here for many yearz. My names Leonie Baus, nice to meet zyou William." Her accent slipping through the more that she tried to pronounce English dialect.

"I've never seen this shop before Leonie. Not to mention the books of folklore you have and the magnificent toys! My children would love this place." William chirped as his eyes wondered around the shop more taking in the scene, still holding onto the book, keeping it close to his chest.

Candy Cane

"I has been here for many a year, zhis place is my home when we moved from our homeland. Zhose bookz are from ma childhood, zhe one you are holding iz ma favourite of zhem all, Krampen." Placing her fragile hands upon the wrapping paper, Leonie's eyes moved from the book to William's curious face as his grip never left the books edge.

"Krampen? Krampus, this is the legendary story of the horned shadow, the one who would punish whilst the other rewarded." William stuttered as his heart skipped a beat, being fascinated by folklore was always his main interest. During his youth he travelled around the world for a year exploring where folklores had originated from, even nonseasonal ones like '*Moth man*' or '*The Goats bridge.*'

"Correct, Krampan would alwayz scare me as a child. Going back to zhe 6th century, Krampus would come along on zhe 6th of December on '*The Krampusnacht,*' but instead of zhe coal, he would punish zhe naughty

Candy Cane

children with whips and chains. If you heard his bell, you knew he was coming for you, to take you away in his basket- dragging you to his underworld." With each word, William's eyes grew wider as a horned shadow took over his own. Feeling a strong connection to the tale, he placed the legendary book upon the table as he leaned in closer to hear more of the tale.

"Wow... I've only ever heard of him being the 'evil Santa,' but this is amazing. I have more respect for Krampus than I do for that jolly fat man." William cooed stroking the leather book, his eyes dripping with excitement.

"Well, if you want zhe book, I could let you has it, but on one condition." Leonie sternly whispered as the light above them flickered. The air seemed to stand still, even the puppets on their strings dared not to move. "Wait really?" William's voice rose above a whisper as his head cracked up towards Leonie's now darkened

Candy Cane

expression, as an unnatural grin formed across her wrinkled old face.

"Zhe story of Krampan is no tale, zhis is the truth. His story has been buried and only zhe special few can break that seal and bring him out. I offer you zhe chance to live zhe life you were meant to live, William Jeffery Nicolas Miller..." Leonie's voice deepened as she held her hands out towards him. Taking a closer look at them under the light, William noticed they had extended; her bones breaking her paper thin skin as if she had claws coming out of her finger tips. The darkened pits of her eyes glowed a yellow shade as her teeth had formed into razor sharp fangs.

"I never told you my full name?" Willam whispered, his body unable to move as fear took hold, freezing him in place.

"Zhis is your time William, zhe Krampan needs a new host, and he has chosen you..." her voice deep and demonic as a horned shadow loomed behind her, the

Candy Cane

bells he heard before becoming louder as if his ear drums would pop.

"What the fuck?" Willaim screamed as he tried to move. Tears pricked the corners of his eyes as he tried desperately to get out, sweat encasing his entire body like a waterfall.

"Zhis is your time William, 'The Krampusnacht' is upon us..." Leonie shouted lunging over the counter towards William, wrapping paper and ribbon exploding across the shop floor. Her claws dug deeper into his arms as his warm coppery blood oozed through the puncture wounds. Her eyes glowed harder as black smoke filled the shop, with the sound of whips dragging across the floor echoing in William's head. His salty tears streamed down his face into his unkept beard, dampening it more mixing with his sweat. Leonie's mouth opened wide showing those razor-sharp teeth. Her head cracked back in an unnatural way as if her neck had just

Candy Cane

snapped, when he heard a deep horn escaping through her gaping mouth.

"William..." A sinister dark voice echoed through the manic noise as Leonie's claws dug deeper, scratching down his forearm as William wiggled under her grasp.

"Please I have a family... no..." William pleaded as he heard the cloved hoofs draw closer to him, his heart pounding against his ribs as if it was going to break free.

His body shook uncontrollably until his eyes shot open, and he sat up in his double bed, his alarm horn blaring as he was drenched in sweat.

Candy Cane

Chapter Five:

'Be naughty. Save Santa the trip...'

"Wa... was that all a dream?" He whispered, sweat seeping more into his bedsheets as his body shook uncontrollably.

Leaning over with shaking hands, he picked up his phone; the time reading **7:00AM**, switching off his alarm quickly unable to bare the sound of the horns. His head ached as if he was hungover from a night out drinking. Gripping the sweat covered duvet corner, William stepped out of bed, his legs still like jelly as he reached down pulling on his moth eaten dark blue dressing gown. Making his way towards his bedroom door, his body felt as if it was hit by a truck full of trauma. His shaking hand rested on the broken doorknob as he could hear the familiar laughter of his two children coming from downstairs.

Candy Cane

"You're okay, it was just a dream... breathe Will, it'll be okay." He comforted himself as he took a big breath in. Closing his eyes, he was unable to get the image of the glowing yellow eyes that burned in his mind, as he exhaled pulling the door towards him and stepping out.

Turning into the narrow hallway, William passed his two children's bedrooms. The ivory white door with blue butterflies belonged to his youngest and only daughter Sidney, and the off-white door with scuff marks all over it belonged to his eldest son, James. The old wooden floorboards creaked under his weight as he approached the white staircase. Holding onto the rusted old banister, William steadied himself down the stairs and towards the source of the laughter, alongside his wife's frustrated groans.

"Can you both just sit down please? And eat your breakfast!" Tilly groaned as she walked around the kitchen in her pristine uniform, her lanyard swaying wildly.

Candy Cane

"Come on James, I need you to get a move on please. Sidney don't touch that, it's a present for your father!" She shouted as William walked through the doorframe and into the chaotic morning scene.

Tilly stood holding up a box wrapped in green and red wrapping paper, covered in mistletoe eerily like the one in his dream. Her mousy blonde hair was pinned up into a messy bun as her small, framed glasses clung to her face; fixed to it, like glue from her makeup. Her crystal blue eyes fixed on her daughter's that matched. Sidney's strawberry blonde hair was shoulder length, so it was easier for her to manage. No one wanted to be fussing around with a seven-year-old when her hair matted, especially this early in the morning.

"But Mommy I want to play with it!" Sidney's high-pitched voice whined.

"Hey now my angel, remember it's almost Christmas you have to be good! Otherwise Santa won't bring you anything." William chirped as he walked over to his

Candy Cane

fussing daughter, her eyes already tearful after being told no.

"I really wish you wouldn't fill their heads with that nonsense!" Tilly sneered as she looked down her nose towards William, her expression one of disgust and frustration.

"What? It's Christmas Tilly, you can't expect me to break their spirits. Just because you're a cold-hearted bitch doesn't mean I have to be." William sneered, his eyes landing on the box held within her hands; the wrapping paper still sending a chill of discomfort down his spine.

"Whatever Will, have this and get out my face. Come on kids, it's time for school!" She screeched, throwing the box towards him as she stormed out of the kitchen; throwing her bag over her shoulder with the car keys jingling in her hand.

Candy Cane

"It's okay Daddy, I still believe." Sidney smiled weakly, placing a kiss on his cheek before running behind her brother and towards the door.

James was only older by four years, his pudgy body wobbling off in the distance. His hair was short and dark black whilst his eyes were an emerald green. His features never resembled William, not one of them, which always had William wondering if he was actually his or not, since James was the only reason they stayed together in their intoxicating marriage. Turning to the boxed present and holding it with shaking hands, an unsettling feeling crept down his spine once more as goosebumps appeared across his arms.

William gripped the box lid pulling it in one motion as he ripped through the wrapping paper, tearing it clean off. The contents made his heart stop, but only for a moment as his tired eyes landed upon the book from his dream. As vivid as his memory would allow him to remember about the nightmare, every detail was the

Candy Cane

exact same; right down to the leather colour, the scuffed buckle and even the cursive writing and illustrations on the front. The golden corners and illustration sparkled under the blaring kitchen light as the red cursive writing read what he feared. '*Krampan.*'

"William..." That deep sinister voice echoed in his ear as if someone or something had just been standing right next to him, sending chills of unease down his spine, making him drop the box.

"No... NO! Get away from me!" His voice broke as he stepped back away from the book, his body trembling as he stared at the box in front of him. His dull blue eyes darted around the room, and upon seeing the trash bag open, he quickly grabbed the box; shoving it inside as he opened the front door. Throwing the black bag into the trash bin outside and rushing back in, he locked the door, panting hard like a dog before heading towards the kitchen to make himself a coffee. Then suddenly, he noticed the book on the table without the

Candy Cane

box, with a handwritten note above it, written in red cursive ink saying;

'Can't get rid of me that easily. The Krampusnacht is soon. The ritual has begun...'

Candy Cane

Chapter Six:

'Christmas comes, but once a year...'

As tears fell down his sweat riddled face, William sat across from the book as if he was a detective interrogating it, like in one of those old black and white 60's films. No matter what he tried to do, it always came back to him, and time had no meaning to him. Whether he was late for work or not, this book needed dealing with.

Still sat in his moth-eaten blue dressing gown, William's phone alarm horn blared again, the time flashing on his screen **7:45AM.** His head pounded as he rested his hand to it, to try and give himself some relief. The book was indestructible. It always came back, from burning it on the stove, throwing it out or burying it in the back yard. It would reappear on his pine wood dining table once again.

Candy Cane

"Why? Why me?" He whimpered as he rested his head on the cold wooden table that still had the breakfast plates scattered across it. The coffee pot had been left on the counter and had been forgotten about, and had now had turned cold.

"William..." That sinister voice echoed through the eerily silent house as the kitchen lights flickered above him.

"What do you want with me?" He cried harder as the lights flickered faster. A gust of wind sent an icy tingle down his spine as a horned shadow appeared across from him, those deep yellow eyes glowing brighter than he remembered.

"We want you... Your Christmas spirit is just like ours... Full of rage and broken, but we can help..." The voice cooed as William lifted his head slightly, staring deep into those eyes he feared.

"You're wrong, it's not broken! Get out of my house, NOW!" He screamed, noticing an empty whisky glass

Candy Cane

bottle to his right. As he picked it up, he threw it towards the shadow, but with no luck it just passed through it like black smoke; smashing against the countertop.

"Your wife doesn't love you... You work a job that doesn't respect you... William... Your holiday spirit has turned to hatred; your heart is black... Continue the ritual let him out... let the naughty ones suffer!" The voice roared as the lights flickered uncontrollably, the kitchen shaking as the wind blew harder.

The leather-bound book slid towards him from the sudden gust of wind as the yellow glowing eyes followed behind it, falling into his sweat encased hands. His body shook from the coldness of the wind, and as he held the book, the leather felt eerily like human skin. His eyes glued upon the book seeing it in his hands as if it was for the first time, and he hadn't noticed how close the horned shadow was now; only inches away from his face.

Candy Cane

"Open the book... Continue the ritual... Make the naughty suffer and let him free... William..." The voice demanded as the wind blew harder, the cold breeze almost turning the room into ice as the windows frosted over from the inside.

"B... but my family? I need to provide for them. I need to..." His voice hoarse from the screaming as his eyes never left the book.

"The boy isn't even yours William... You know that is true, he's nothing like you... Open the book and you'll see the truth she'd been hiding... Open the book and continue the ritual... The girl will be safe..." Taunting him, the voice whispered in his ear, so close it felt like he could feel breath on his neck as goosebumps appeared once again.

"You promise Sidney will be safe?" He whimpered again as his eyes lifted for a second to stare at the deep yellow eyes, that were now right in front of his nose. He had been so preoccupied by holding the ancient

Candy Cane

book that he hadn't noticed how close the shadow had got to him.

"If she is good, she won't be harmed... the naughty ones William... The naughty must be punished... Open the book and continue the ritual... He must be freed to correct the cosmic mistakes... Do it William..." The voice roared as wind blew harder. The disregarded plates from the morning breakfast were sent tumbling to the floor as they smashed on impact.

"As long as she won't be harmed..." He whispered. His shaking hand from the sudden cold gripped the icy cold, golden buckle as he lifted the front cover. The wind blazed uncontrollably as the sound of bells and cloven hooves echoed through the kitchen, as a horn rang through his ears. The shadow lunged towards him, and the last thing he saw were the deep yellow eyes merging into his own; his chair falling backwards onto the cold laminated flooring— and then everything went black.

Candy Cane

Candy Cane

Chapter Seven:

'Sorry Santa, Naughty Just Feels Nice...'

Hours passed as the morning glow now turned to the afternoon rays. The kitchen sat untouched as the smashed plates and whisky bottle still lay scattered across the floor and countertop. The windows were smeared with condensation as William's body sat stiffly on the chair on the laminated floor, his body ice cold as the book lay open beside him.

The front door opened with a sharp '*click*' as the sound of heels against the wooden floor rushed through the still house. William didn't move as his wife made her way towards the Kitchen entrance, her bag slamming against the pine table as she saw the ungodly mess.

"William! What the fuck did you do? Have you been drinking again?" She shrieked, noticing the whisky bottle shattered across the countertop. With anger

Candy Cane

seeping out of her mouth, she looked around the kitchen where she had only been a few hours prior.

Stepping towards William's cold body she kicked his leg gently, and he made no movement as she sighed in frustration. Storming away, Tilly grabbed the dustpan as she started to gather all of the broken pieces of glass and porcelain from the plates; slicing her hand open with a small shard. Her skin sliced easily like paper as her dark red blood oozed out of it, dripping onto the floor. The copper smell made William's eyes shoot open, his eyes bloodshot as he looked around. His vision was blurred, and the only thing he could remember was opening the book as the faint sound of bells jingled in the back of his head. Rolling over to his right side, his eyes landed onto the book as his memory came rushing back, the horned shadow, the yellow glowing eyes, what they said to him. He opened the book, he needed to continue the ritual, but what did that entail?

Candy Cane

"Ow! Fucking idiot, why the fuck did I marry this lazy piece of shit... God's sake this hurts like a motherfucker!" Tilly grunted as she placed her wounded hand under the cold running water, wincing as the water made contact with her split skin. The muscle underneath it pulsed as more blood flowed out of it, mixing with the clear water seeping down the drain.

"You're home early..." William's voice croaked as he lifted his hand up onto the table to try and steady himself, seeing his wife hunched over the kitchen sink, with blood staining her pristine uniform.

"Oh, so you're awake now! I've just cut my hand open because of the mess you made you drunken dick. Why didn't you go to work?" Tilly screeched as she grabbed the ivory tea towel, wrapping her wounded hand in it as her blood stained the innocent towel. Tilly winced as the fibres of the towel sunk into the gash in her palm. She stared at him, hatred filling her eyes as she held back tears of pain.

Candy Cane

"I'm not drunk, you didn't answer my question Tilly. Why are you back home early?" William sternly said as he approached her slowly, the book left open on the ground.

"I came home for my lunch you idiot, but instead I need to clean up your fucking mess! Why didn't you go to work?" She shouted back, her anger exploding through her voice as she gestured around the room.

William stood staring at Tilly, his face expressionless as the bells overpowered any thought he tried to process. His eyes glanced around the kitchen as the light started to flicker slowly again, and the rage he felt all these years had started to bubble under his skin as if he was about to pop. The faint sounds of chains being dragged down the far stairs made his heart pound harder, like hooves against the gravel path. His eye twitched as he tried to keep his temper under control, feeling as if it was slipping from his grip.

Candy Cane

"Have you been fired because of the incident yesterday at the mall with that manager? I told you not to go for that job. Yet again you ignored me and went anyway, embarrassing me in the process. You fucking moron!" Tilly screamed, spit flying out of her mouth as she stared at William's cold expression.

"You have no right to scream at me anymore Tilly. I have not been fired. I do everything for this family and yet you still undermine me!" William spoke, voice dark as his eyes locked onto Tilly's; his face still and cold. The spit that had landed on his cheek just sat there, and he didn't move to wipe it away.

"William Jeffery Nicholas Miller, you will listen to me, I am your wife. You need to snap out of this idiotic mindset and get your ass in the real world! Stop thinking about this stupid holiday and the crappy folklore shit you followed when you were young, wasting your time on it!" Tilly shouted as more spit

Candy Cane

came flying out of her mouth towards William, drenching him in it.

Glancing towards the opened book, Tilly stormed past William; knocking his shoulder as she bent down picking up the leather-bound book, her face a mixture of anger and disgust. Her hand wrapped around the binding as she inspected it closely, bringing it to her face more as she readjusted her glasses for a better view. Her eyes widening as fear crept in her hand, trembling slightly as she turned to William.

"I gave you a stupid box I had as a secret Santa, and this is what was inside it? Another book of folklore crap! You better not be infesting our children's minds with this nonsense, and what is it even made from, it is disgusting?!" Tilly said, gagging whilst she smelt the rotting book.

"Put the book down." William sternly shouted as he slowly walked towards her, his hand behind his back hidden from view.

Candy Cane

"William stop acting childishly, it's just a fucking book. I'm throwing it away. It's disgusting and I don't want my children infested with some disease that could come from it." She sneered as she gripped the books spine. Heading towards the trash bin and turning her back on William, he launched forward, knocking her to the ground. Her glasses flew off her face as she squirmed from under his weight.

"I said put the book down you whore." He whispered in her ear as he pulled her up by her hair, his voice a deep growl as he smashed her head back into the ground, bursting her nose as blood sprayed everywhere.

Candy Cane

Chapter Eight:

'Santa's got the toys, Krampus has... other plans.'

"Will... please..." Tilly choked as her own blood filled her lungs, her nose completely mangled, trying to breathe as she was gurgling.

The wet slaps of her head colliding with the floor filled the room, as animalistic growls flooded out of Williams mouth. Blood sprayed across the kitchen floor, walls and cupboards as Tilly's body became limp. She didn't make another sound, not even a whimper of pain. Dropping her blood-soaked head into the massive puddle on the floor, William retreated to the far corner; his hands on his head as he saw what he had done. The once love of his life, who he would've done anything for now faceless, and her body lay in a puddle of her own blood. Tears pricked his eyes as he looked onto his hands. A dark crimson blood dripped from

Candy Cane

them as he noticed his fingers had changed, longer and sharper; just like the old woman's in his nightmare.

"What... what happened?" His voice soft as tears glided down his face, his body shaking as he stared at his warm blood covered hands.

"The naughty one was punished... That's part of the ritual... Another will be home soon... Keep going William." The sinister voice whispered in his head as he rocked back and forth, his body and mind breaking from the trauma.

Standing up shakily, William stepped over his lifeless wife's body as he picked up the book soaked in blood, as he opened it once more. His body moved as if it was on auto pilot as he sat across from his mangled wife's face. He flipped the first page over, seeing that it was called '*Naughty List*' as he picked up a shard of glass, dipping the end in the blood puddle. William proceeded to write her name under '*Naughty List*,' using the blood like red ink as the glass shard connected to the paper.

Candy Cane

"I'm sorry Tilly, but you needed to be a sacrifice. You won't be alone soon, my love..." William cooed as he stroked her blood-soaked blonde hair. Placing the book back onto the table, he sprinted up the stairs, the floorboards crackling wildly like whips as he pulled down the attic door; the metal stairs falling hard against the floor with a loud '*thud.*'

Climbing up the rusted old metal ladders, his wife's blood still stained his hands as he poked his head into the darkened attic space, fumbling around for what felt like ages. William eventually found the string connected to the light as he pulled it down slightly. A small bulb just above his head illuminated the room as he jumped over boxes that were covered in asbestos and cobwebs. A large dark green box encased in a year's worth of dust and cobwebs sat in the far corner, alongside dark brown boxes labelled '*X-mas Decks.*'

Box after box came tumbling down the old metal stairs as William ran back and forth, until he hoisted the large

Candy Cane

darkened green one towards the attic opening. He gently carried it down the stairs as he followed after it. Signing deeply, he began to take the dust covered boxes down the stairs. The floorboard creaked as he scurried up and down the stairs, carrying box after box and setting them down in the small living room to the left of the front door. His deceased wife still lay in her now crusted over blood that had seeped into the kitchen floor.

"Time to decorate, the children will be home soon..." William chuntered, as he unboxed the large green box first; setting up the Christmas tree in the far corner.

Candy Cane

Chapter Nine:

'You better watch out. You better not cry...'

More hours passed as William buzzed around the house, getting his decorations ready for the children's arrival. Multicoloured tinsel had been strung up along the banister to the stairs as the tree stood tall, already plugged into the wall. The green and red lights made the tree's branches sparkle, feeling the festive cheer; the monster inside of him needing something darker.

Walking into the kitchen, William rustled through the cabinet draw pulling out a butcher's knife. Setting it down on the counter, he whipped around on his heels to face his wife's remains as he kicked her; just as she did him. She didn't move. Sighing again, he bent down wrapping his claw like fingers, still encased in her blood around her cold ankles. Pulling her closer to him, he

Candy Cane

flipped her onto her back getting a better look at her face; or what was left of it.

Her nose was completely mangled. Her face was covered in black bruises and marks where her skin had torn from the impact, but the killing blow was her nose bone fracturing off and puncturing through to her brain. Her left eye was completely bloodshot while her other had formed a particularly nasty black eye. Suffocating on her own blood as she was dying, Tilly's face took on a slight blue hue as well as the blacken bruises, and blood stained clothing.

"My poor girl, if you weren't such a whore and cheated on me, I wouldn't have done this. I know he's not mine. He will be joining you soon..." William spat on her blood covered face as he moved a singular strand of loose hair out from her face.

Gripping her blood stained blouse, William ripped it in two instantly as the buttons cascaded to the ground like the sound of teeth being knocked out. Showing her

Candy Cane

laced designer bra hiding her small chest, he stared for a moment, disgust falling upon himself again as he grabbed the butcher's knife from the counter. Raising it high above him, he swung it down onto her abdomen. Fresh cold blood trickled out of the gash in her stomach as her body made no movement, no sound came from her, just silence.

Reaching his hand into the recently made gash in her abdomen, William fished around with her internal organs, like a child playing with their favourite toy as he gripped onto both intestines; ripping them from her body and out the gash. Running towards the living room with them in hand, he began wrapping them like garlands around his tree. William stood back and admired the blood glistening off his once festive tree, and as he tilted his head to the left, his head pinged with an idea as he grinned wickedly. Rushing back to his wife's mutilated corpse, he picked up a spoon as he forced it into her puffy eye socket, swirling it around until he heard a *'pop'* as the eyeball dangled from the

Candy Cane

optical nerve. Leaning down and inspecting his work, he smiled wildly as he picked up the eyeball with his mouth as he pulled hard. Eventually, the optical nerve gave out– snapping as yellow puss oozed out of the snapped nerve. Spitting the clouded saliva covered eye back into his blood encrusted hand, flakes of red slipped off from him as he lifted the mushy ball to his own eyes; inspecting it. The optical nerve, or what was left of it, dangled from the severed eyeball leaking the yellow and clumpy puss; like a faucet running water. Shuffling towards the living room with his new decoration, William placed the eyeball onto the glistening green tree, now dripping with crimson red liquid and clumpy puss.

Candy Cane

Chapter Ten:

'Jingle all the Way...'

Blood splattered the walls as if giving them a fresh coat of paint as William rushed up the ever-creaking staircase. Going through his bedroom door with such force it almost came off it's hinges, he ripped open his wardrobe. With his wife's phone clutched in his left-hand and vibrating like crazy, the smashed screen read **3:35PM**. The children were due to be picked up any moment, and he needed to be there.

"Shit, shit, shit! I need to be there now." He mumbled panicking as he pulled out clothes, scattering them across the bed as he dug deeper into his wardrobe. Finally, he pulled out a black crumpled old shirt and some blue denim jeans that seemed to not have seen the light of day for decades.

Ripping off his sweat and blood coated dressing gown, he ran towards the bathroom turning the cold mould

Candy Cane

infested faucet on; ice cold water running from it as the temperature slowly began heating up. William scrubbed his dust and blood covered hands, watching the water turn from clear to a darkened crimson. Looking towards his reflection in the musty mirror, William's eyes seemed more sunken into his face as his dull blue eyes now had a hint of yellow hidden behind them. His cheekbone protruded more as his beard seemed a little longer, producing a couple of stray white hairs within the brown.

"What the fuck?" He whispered staring into his reflection for a moment, slightly mortified by himself. His wife's broken phone vibrated once again against the cluttered bed, snapping him out of his thoughts as he rushed about grabbing his worn-out black boots.

With the jingle of his keys, William headed towards the door. Within seconds he was on the stairs, the melody of creaking as he glided down them, stopping every now and again admiring his own handy work. The

Candy Cane

D.I.Y. decorations using his wife's dead carcass as parts for his ritualistic, seasonal decoration around his home.

"They're going to love this, I know *he* does." He cooed as his voice deepened slightly. Walking towards the front door, William slammed it behind him rushing to his beat up, rusted old truck.

Backing out of his small driveway, Tilly's silver Mercedes- bought with her daddy's money, sat shimmering in the afternoon sun that hid behind the dull white clouds. Driving down the roads, his truck spitting blackened smoke from its broken exhaust, roaring and begging to have it fixed. The truck itself making a strange humming sound that had been completely ignored for years. Arriving outside the bright green gates of the school, the engine roared and spat as William coasted around, trying to find somewhere to park the death trap of a truck. Finally, after what felt like years, William squeezed the ungodly loud truck in

Candy Cane

between two smaller ones; turning the key and letting the engine rest before it overheated.

The door squeaked as he wiggled out from behind it, his boots crunching on the dried fallen leaves as he strolled towards the glistening green gates. His keys jingled in his freshly cleaned hands, as he smiled at the other parents patiently waiting for their children, trying to act normal; as normal as he could even, if their eyes were glued upon him. His confident domineer never changed as the bells started again in the back of his mind, his heart pounding as sweat slightly formed on his brow. Whispers glided through the crowd of patient waiting adults as he shifted uncomfortably in his spot, the bells getting louder almost drowning out his own thoughts again.

"Why is he here? Where's Tilly?" a woman whispered holding her leather purse closely to her body as she leaned over to who must have been her friend.

Candy Cane

"I don't know, but she never misses pick up. It's like her gossip time, since we never get to see her with him constantly being a lazy twat." The other woman whispered as they both giggled and snickered, pointing at the apparel and sharing glances to the other parents.

"*Naughty... The Ritual...*" The sinister voice whispered in his ear as the bells rang harder in his head. The wind blew colder as William screwed his hand into a fist, trying to keep his calm.

"Not now, they will have their time." He whispered back, shaking his head slightly as his eyes landed on the far opening school doors; sighing in relief as the bells softened, and hearing the children's laughter echoing through the gusts of wind.

Candy Cane

Chapter Eleven:

'Christmas Magic is in the air...'

As the whispers dissipated, the sound of children's screams of joy travelled within the cold breeze as their school shoes ran on the gravelled path towards the green gates of freedom. Teachers followed behind like herding sheep, whistles blew loud trying to capture their attention for the last time; and a ragged old teacher made her way through the nest of children as she pulled a long, golden key from her pocket. Unlocking the gates, the children spilled out to their parents.

"Single file now, remember to be careful!" Her voice screeched as she watched each child go to their respected parent, her misted eyes hidden behind her half-framed glasses as her pointed nose kept them on her face.

Watching all the children run to their parents made William's stomach turn, and the realisation of his

Candy Cane

daughter never seeing her mother again pained him; yet gave him satisfaction that she would never see the evil that was inside of her- to poison her, and make her like her mother. She was the first to be given to the ritual, and what would be a greater sacrifice than the one he loved the most? Even if they were a lying, cheating scumbag.

"Mr. Miller, so nice to see you after so long." The ragged teacher said with a slight smirk. William was so lost in thought that he didn't notice her approach him.

"Ah, Ms. Stonely yes, it has been some time hasn't it." William smiled, scratching the back of his head, his heart pounding as the overwhelming smell of Ms. Stonely's perfume invaded his nostrils. With her greying hair tied up in a high pony, her arms slumped by her sides as her school lanyard swung slightly from the cool breeze.

"Where is your wife? Doesn't she usually do pick up?" Ms. Stonely questioned as she peaked around behind

Candy Cane

him to see if she was hiding in the ever-growing group of children and parents around them.

"She wasn't feeling well, bit of an upset stomach." William staggered as he pushed himself into her view, his smile wiry as the sweat on his brow began to fall. "So naturally I told her to go to bed and that I'd pick up James and Sidney today." He smiled again trying to throw her off his trail.

"Oh, I do hope she'll be okay. Give her my love won't you? I won't keep you any longer, but you should know James got into an altercation today with Timmy again." Ms. Stonely sighed as she rested her hand on his arm, stroking it slightly before bringing her arm back. Her voice sounding concerned as she spoke about the incident.

"Again? What did he do this time?" William growled as his anger brewed in his voice.

"They were on the playground I believe, and someone hit someone- then before I knew it, they were in my

Candy Cane

office and Timmy had a blackened eye with a nosebleed. I hate to say this Mr. Miller, but if this carries on, we will have to think about exclusion or expelling young James, as he is a hazard to the other children." Her voice was sharp as she tried to console William, however this only made the anger inside of him bubble more, alongside the bells chiming harder at each piece of news he heard.

Just on queue, James wobbled beside Ms. Stonely as his green eyes looked William up and down with that same look his wife would've given him, disgust. His blackened hair was covered in sweat as his fat body panted hard; the walk from the school doors must have taken all his energy away. His knuckle gripped his bag on his shoulder that was covered in black and purple bruises, probably from the fight he started earlier no doubt. Rolling his green eyes, he turned to see what must have been Timmy slither out of the green gates. His crystal blue eyes pierced through the blackened one that had swollen, as his nose was as red as Rudolph's; not

Candy Cane

because of the cold weather, but because it was still probably irritated. His blonde hair was scruffy with little bits of twigs or leaves sticking out, as his eyes panicked looking around for his parents.

"Fucking pathetic loser." James ruff voice spat as he slowly walked towards Timmy, as William was busy trying to prove Ms. Stonely he was innocent.

"Oi Timmy, who you looking for? Your mommy?" James mocked as he pushed Timmy back into the school gates making, his drop his bag to the floor.

"Please, J... James leave me alone! Ha... haven't you hurt m... me enough today?" Timmy begged in between sobs, as he held his arms up to protect himself trembling with fear.

"I don't care you cry baby! You're nothing but a mommy's boy! So where is she now, huh?" James mocked as he snorted, holding his hands up looking around briefly.

Candy Cane

Laughing to himself, James lifted his right fist up ready to land a blow again onto Timmy when he felt something hit the back of his head hard; making him stagger for a second, but just long enough for Timmy to crawl out of his defenceless corner. Grabbing his bag as he cried hard, he ran off to the adults in the far corner of the parking lot in hopes of finding help.

"Ugh, what the fuck was that?" James croaked as he turned around, stroking the back of his head where he was just hit by something– or someone.

"James, just stop it now." Sidney's sweet, innocent voice cooed as she held her bag in both of her hands, panting hard.

"Sid, you fucking idiot." James shouted as he tackled her to the ground, her head hitting the gravel with a loud '*thud*,' stunning her in place. His right fist clenched hard as his other was entangled in her strawberry blonde hair, pulling it hard as he felt bits of her scalp tearing away from her head.

Candy Cane

"James, stop you're hurting me please!" Sidney pleaded as tears stained her face, blood oozing down into her vision from the bits of scalp being forcefully torn from her head.

"No. You always get away with everything, you should've just let me take my anger out on Timmy." He shouted as he leaned down, pulling her up by her hair as he reached her ear. "But now I'll just take my anger out on you!" He whispered, laughing sinisterly as he slammed her hand back down onto the gravel path. More tears expelled out of Sidney's eyes, and she screamed tearing her little voice box in the process.

"Where's mommy? Help please!" Sidney screamed as her voice came out hoarse, blood blinding her vison as she felt her hair be torn away from her head as the exposed skin burned against the cold breeze.

"Ms. Stonely I completely understand, and I am so sorry about today, but I promise you we will have a talk with James and..." His sentence was cut off at the blood

Candy Cane

chilling screams, his heart stopping as he looked behind Ms. Stonely to see his daughter being literally torn apart by the fat bastard that wasn't even his.

"Sidney!" He shouted as he pushed Ms. Stonely out the way running towards his daughters cries for help, his blood boiling as anger fuelled him. A small group had formed around the fight, with both parents and children looking at what was happening; but not stepping in to get the large creature off the young vulnerable girl. A small pool of blood gathered under Sidney's head as she cried harder, clawing into James's hand to let her hair go as a desperate attempt to get him off, but it was no use.

"James Miller! Let her go!" William roared as he pushed the small group apart finally getting to his children; his anger on the verge of over exposure as he gripped the collar of James uniform, using all of his strength to pull him away from the wounded Sidney.

Candy Cane

"Daddy!" Sidney quivered as she looked up at him, covered in blood and tears as she shook uncontrollably, adrenaline and trauma seeping into her system.

"What the fuck? We were having fun!" James laughed as William kept hold of his collar, not daring to let him go.

"Fun? FUN! You almost killed your sister and that's fun? And Timmy?" William shouted as he threw James to the ground hard, standing over Sidney like a lion protecting its young cub.

"So, you're the one who hurt my Timmy?" A familiar voice shouted from the ever-growing crowd of teachers, parents and fellow classmates.

Turning to see who the face was to the voice, a chill ran down William's spine as he recognised the thick framed glasses and blonde hair tied up in a high ponytail; the deep scratch marks on her arm and face plastered with makeup. It was Susan Jones- the manager from the mall.

Candy Cane

"No wonder that child is a menace, with a father like you, who wouldn't be?!" Her voice was sharp like glass as she spat her venom. Timmy hid behind her like a frightened deer.

"Look I'm sorry about the other day at the mall, but this has nothing to do with me!" William apologised as he reached down to help Sidney up who was still shaking like a leaf, holding the pieces of scalp her brother had ripped from her.

"Nothing to do with you? Don't make me laugh. He is a monster, a menace! Look what he did to my poor Timmy and your daughter. Like father like son, I suppose!" Susan scoffed as she clung onto her own son as if someone was going to take him away from her at a moment's notice.

"He's not my dad you crazy bitch!" James shouted as he stood back up whipping the dust from his trousers.

Candy Cane

"What are you on about you delusional boy?" Susan questioned as her grip grew tighter on Timmy, her acrylic nails digging into his already wounded skin.

"He's not my dad; Mom had an affair and only married him for his money. She told me not to say anything, but I've had enough of playing happy fucking family." He scowled, looking towards William clutching onto his wounded daughter.

"Let's hope Santa brings you more that fucking coal for Christmas you ungrateful little monster, as for you Mr. Miller I am truly sorry. Come on Timmy let's leave this shit show." Susan shouted as she leaned over, picking her precious boy up and taking him away as the crowd of people gasped and fell silent watching the drama unfold.

"Sidney, my angel, are you okay?" William cooed at his swaying daughter, who's complexion had grown from pale to worryingly white.

Candy Cane

"I... I'm okay Da.. Daddy, can we go ho... home now?" She whispered as her eyelids became heavy, losing that much blood her body was shutting down in need of sleep- or a concussion overriding her thoughts. Her little body needed to be home and resting, instead of being some sick drama show for everyone to be looking at.

"Yes sweetie, we will be going home now." William cooed as he swept her up in his arms, cradling her like the baby she was to him, as the bells began their cruel melody in his head. Every step he took sounded like cloven hoofs against the gravel path.

"James, get in the fucking truck, NOW!" William shouted his voice deepening as the onlookers separated like Moses with the red sea, watching every move the three of them made intensely; the tension you could cut with a knife.

"Don't worry Sidney, we will be home soon." William whispered to her as she passed out in his arms, his

Candy Cane

anger on overload as he heard the sinister voices again taunting him in his mind.

Candy Cane

Chapter Twelve:

'Chestnuts roasting on an open fire...'

"We told you so... That he wasn't yours... Go home and continue the ritual... he's waiting..." The sinister voices sang along with the bells taunting melody as William's body stopped. Reaching the truck, his anger radiated off him like toxic waste.

"D... Dad? Can you unlock the truck door?" James stuttered as he stood behind him, his voice still rough yet sounding like a child that knows they were in trouble.

Ignoring the noise behind him, William pushed him out of the way as he unlocked the truck, placing Sidney down on the passenger's side of the truck. As he placed her backpack underneath her head to elevate it slightly, he inspected what James had done to his precious girl. Three large parts of her scalp had been torn from her head, bleeding profusely as the gash in her head bled

Candy Cane

more from where he had been slamming it against the gravel path, as bits of gravel and small sticks were embedded in her skull.

"You sick fucker, I'll make you fucking pay." William whispered through gritted teeth as he whipped around closing the truck door shut. He placed his hands around James's neck, his eyes burning with anger; the glow of yellow slowly making their way over his dull blue shade.

"Listen here you disturbed fuck, when we get home things will change. *YOU* will change! Do you understand me?" William spat as his grip grew tighter, James's complexion turning a shade of blue as his airway was slowly being crushed by the sheer pressure of anger in William's grip.

"O... okay!" James managed to conjure up as he clung onto William's arms trying to breathe.

Throwing the fat boy into his truck making it sway slightly, William walked over to his driver side as he opened the door. Placing himself down gently to not

Candy Cane

disturb Sidney, he heard James gasps for air in the back; his anger still emanating from him as he turned the engine on. The engine spat and curdled until it turned over and roared. Setting the gear into drive, he hit the car in front of him without caring as he sped off home. The car ride was silent for the most part, apart from the odd coughing from James who was still trying to breathe properly.

Arriving outside their home, the twinkle of Christmas lights sparkled through the pulled down blinds as James noticed his mother's Mercedes still parked outside the house. His mood changed from fear to safe as he knew his mother wouldn't let this man hurt him anymore. His excitement got the better of him as he sprinted out of the busted old truck, running towards the front door. Little did he know what he was about to see would change his world forever. James gripped the handle of the door as it opened with ease, his excitement overwhelming, and he didn't notice the small splash of blood over the corner of the door as he stepped inside.

Candy Cane

"Mom I'm home! You won't believe what that fucker has done to me!" His voice shouted as it broke slightly after being strangled by William; his throat still sore.

With no answer from Tilly, James walked around the entrance before he headed towards the kitchen. William came in not long after, still cradling Sidney in his arms as he lay her down on the sofa and draped a blanket over her resting injured body. Walking back towards the front door, William locked the door leaving his key in the lock as he bolted it with the chain above, where James couldn't reach it. As he slowly approached the kitchen, his anger itched under his skin as he felt it ready to escape. The sound of bells echoed in his mind as the chains he heard before scraped across the floorboards behind him; his body aching as he felt the urge to continue the ritual again.

"*Naughty...*" The sinister voice rang in his ears as he stepped through the doorway of the kitchen, his eyes

Candy Cane

landing on the book as it flipped open to the *'Naughty List.'*

"Mom? Are you in here?" James's voice rang as he carelessly stepped over the pool of crusted blood, where his mothers' body was only hours prior. He hadn't noticed it.

"James?" His mothers voice rang from the living room, however it didn't sound the same. It sounded more distorted and deeper than usual. Without a doubt, he followed it again not noticing William close behind him holding a blood coated knife behind his back.

"James? I'm in the living room. Come to Mommy!" The voice shouted from the other room as James ran across the room, tripping on something as he came tumbling to the ground.

"Ah what the fuck?" He mumbled as he looked back in confusion, seeing his mother's thin framed glasses under his foot. The lenses were smashed as he picked

Candy Cane

them up, noticing a small speck of dried blood on the left lens.

Shakily picking up his mother's broken glasses, James crawled towards the living room; feeling uneasy he peaked his head around the glistening room. He could see Christmas decorations littering every inch of the walls, from tinsel to snowflakes dripping from the ceiling. Yet something still felt off to him, something wasn't right. Where was his mother? And why didn't she have her glasses on?

"Mom?" James said quivering as he heard laughter coming from the room, his nerves getting the better of him as he shook in his boots. Shuffling towards the Christmas tree where it felt safe, he didn't notice the blood dripping onto his shoulder.

His curiosity drew him towards the Christmas tree as he noticed something staring at him, a new bauble his mother must have bought. He didn't recognise it from last year, and the perfectly round bauble shimmered

Candy Cane

under the lights of the tree. He couldn't quite make out the image on the front of it as it was too dull to make out from far away. Picking up the bauble with one hand, it felt slimy, yet firm as if something had spilled on it. Turning it over, he notice red lines that almost looked like veins all around it and his eyes glanced up to see how it was connected to the tree. A red string connected the bauble to the tree, yet it didn't look right again. His curiosity grew fonder as James pulled the firm bauble in his hands. Something musty dripped on his hand as he looked down, thick yellow puss seeping from the slight tear in the optical nerve as he jumped back, feeling disgusted bile rise in his mouth.

"Ew, what the fuck is that?" James shouted, wiping the puss on his trousers as he swallowed down the bile in his mouth. As he properly looked around the tree, horror kept him in place as he saw what he had missed.

Candy Cane

Intestines were draped across the tree like tinsel and more internal organs hung from the tree like Christmas baubles. Blood alongside puss and stomach acid dripped from it, encasing the lights in some sick way that they looked enchanting. Skin draped over boxes like wrapping paper under the tree, as bones gathered like firewood by the chimney. Finally on top of the tree sat the star herself, Tilly's decapitated head; dripping blood as her empty eye socket oozed puss from the severed optical nerve. Her face was still mangled from her broken nose, still frozen in the fear and torment that she went through before her brutal death. Blood danced down the tree as James stood terrified, tears cascading down his face as he stared at his mother- or what was left of her.

"M... Mommy?" James squealed as he stood holding her glasses, his fear planting him in his spot. He couldn't move a muscle, and he was frozen in fear.

Candy Cane

William snuck up behind the frightened boy as he looked at his own work, smirking. As he pulled the blood encased knife from behind his back, the bells rang louder as he heard the voices whisper in his ear, *"The ritual needs another to proceed..."*

"Do you like it?" William's voice was now deeper and darker as he asked James, his hand resting on his shoulder that had now grown longer and sharper like claws; digging into the boy's shoulder and taunting his skin as he broke it slightly.

Candy Cane

Chapter Thirteen:

'Bring your holiday spirit home with you...'

James's skin split almost instantly under the pressure of the nail on his shoulder as blood trickled down his arm. Too stunned to react, his green eyes were glossy as tears glazed over them; his eyes still fixated on his mother's dismembered corpse, and staring into her beaten face. The Christmas lights of green and red danced on her pale face, still stained with her own blood.

"M... Mommy?" James whispered again, his voice breaking as he clung onto her broken glasses. A small shard of her cracked lens embedded itself into his hand as he ignored the searing pain in his shoulder from the nail digging deeper into his tender skin.

Candy Cane

"What's wrong James? She's there!" William mocked, his voice darker as he bent down beside him. His nails dug through each layer of his skin, tearing through his muscle as his copper smelling dark blood drove down his body, staining his once clean and innocent uniform crimson red.

"Sh... she's not..." James mumbled as the pain of his shoulder and the heartbreak made his knees buckle, seeing the only woman he actually cared about slaughtered and strung up like a piece of meat.

It was too much for the young boy to bear as his mind broke, tears expelling from his green eyes as he sobbed and wailed. If you listened hard enough you could physically hear his heart breaking into a million pieces as he curled up into a ball on the floor, cradling his mother's broken glasses and holding them close to his chest. His eyes were red raw as blood vessels invaded every corner of them, and due to his dramatic fall to the floor, William's nail unhooked itself from its place in

Candy Cane

James's shoulder. William stood completely stunned at the scene unfolding in front of him, seeing the boy who had just savagely beaten and nearly killed his own sister. He was curled up like a toddler that wanted its mother and throwing a temper tantrum.

"*William... He is waiting...*" The sinister voices rang in his ears as he watched his son, or rather his ex-wife's son throw a pity party on the floor, almost making him feel sorry for him. *Almost.*

"Who's the cry-baby now? Fucking pathetic. I mean come on James, really?" William mocked whilst holding his arms out to the side, the knife shimmering with crimson under the sparkling lights. James wailed harder as he peaked up towards William's darkened expression. He knew this was the end, and yet he didn't care.

"Just do it..." James sighed in defeat as he buried his head in his arms.

Candy Cane

"Excuse me?" William questioned, caught off guard and puzzled as he sat on the ground watching the boy who had attempted to murder his sister not long ago.

The room fell deadly silent as William watched how broken James had become. It had only taken seeing his mother's body strung up on the tree to break the young boy's mind and soul. Watching him closely something seemed off, for a boy who never showed his emotions- why now? Why when he saw his mother's corpse did he break down now?

"He's tricking you William... Continue the ritual... make him pay..." The sinister voice cooed into his ear as he felt his neck hair stand up, feeling the breeze behind him once more. He gripped the knife hard, noticing that James's eyes seemed to have stopped leaking.

"James, why now? You never showed any emotion before apart from hate, but when you've seen your whore of a mother..." William sneered before being cut off mid sentence by James.

Candy Cane

"She was not a whore! I loved my mom, but now she's gone, and you took her from me!" James screamed, his voice still hoarse from the strangling earlier as he projected his fat orbed body towards William. Launching towards him, what William failed to see was the small bit of broken rib bone James had managed to slip up his sleeve from when he collapsed to the ground, pretending to be frightened.

"You little shit, you tricked me!" William coughed as his body flew backwards onto the carpeted floor. James pinned him with his fat body as he held the broken piece of ivory bone to his neck, his face like thunder.

"I'll make you pay for taking her away, I'll hurt you just enough so you can see me finally kill that little bitch in the corner." James scowled as he locked eyes with William's, his eyes emanating fury as William's eyes started to produce a small yellow hue around them; the bells becoming much louder as a wicked grin grew across William's face.

Candy Cane

"Gotcha!" William's voice whispered as it grew deeper and more distorted, his eyes now fully yellow and glowing wildly as his grin grew wider. Behind James was William's left arm, with the knife pointed to his lower back as he drove the blood stained utensil deep into the boy's fat tissue. Blood pooled out of the gash as he did it twice more.

James screamed in terror and pain as the burning sensation grew too much for him, his eyes glossy as tears strolled down his face. Falling backwards, he lost grip of the rib bone watched it roll under the horror lit Christmas tree as he clung onto his mother's glasses. The sharp lens cut deep into his palm as he tried to crawl away, leaving behind a messy smear line made from his own blood. Trying desperately to get away, William let out a deep animalistic growl as the bells became louder, gripping the dripping knife in one hand. Straddling the young boys back, with his other hand he gripped a tuft of his blackened hair and pulled him up. Feeling the tension in his spine, he knew that if he

Candy Cane

wanted to, he could snap it right then and there make it a quick, swift end to James's torture; but where would be the fun in that?

"Who's the mommy's boy now? You pathetic cry-baby bitch, say hi to Mommy. We'll keep a seat for you to visit at Christmas." William whispered into James's ear as he rose the knife high above his head, towards his crown where his hairline began. He pressed down on the blood-soaked knife, scalping the young boy's hair off as James's scream echoed through the house. All William heard was the familiar bells jingling heavily in his ears as he growled louder, until the screams stopped.

Candy Cane

Chapter Fourteen:

'Make it a December to remember...'

Williams face was covered in streaks of blood as James's still body hung by a slither of skin, still attached to his head from his scalped hair. William sat still straddling him, holding his black hair with his scalp in one hand while in the other dripped in blood; as if he had dipped his hand into strawberry jam. Blood clots dripped from his arm to the blood stained ground.

"That's what you call Karma, no coal for you this Christmas, you spoiled brat!" William panted as he felt the remaining piece of scalp snap in his hand, the lifeless body fell to the ground; blood spraying across the floor as if he had just smashed a watermelon. James's heart had given out halfway through the scalping and due to the sheer terror of it all; it was all too much for his little heart to take.

Candy Cane

The whispers grew louder as the bells stopped their chiming, and a gust of wind caught William's neck as he felt as if someone- or something was stood behind him. Not feeling scared for the first time, he embraced the feeling as he held his arms high; the blood trickling down his body, smiling widely as some bits dripped into his mouth. His heavy eyelids fluttered closed as he tasted the iron in the blood mixed with his saliva, letting the flavours dance on his pallet. He closed his eyes allowing ecstasy take hold of him, *just for a moment.*

"Another one down... Another key unlocked... he's almost free... Don't stop now William..." The sinister voice echoed, snapping him out of his moment of triumph as he smirked, wiping his mouth leaving a bloody smear across it.

With the blooded scalp still in hand, William walked towards the Kitchen and looked towards the opened book. Using the knife tip encased in blood, he used it to inscribe James's name, written underneath his mother's

Candy Cane

name on the '*Naughty List.*' Dropping the murder tool next to the book as he slammed it shut, he felt a sense of relief as he stared across to his still sleeping daughter. Walking back over to her, his hands looked as if he was wearing thick, wet red gloves as William stared at her intensely.

"I'll make sure you're safe my turtledove." He whispered, placing his bloody hand on her matted hair. William looked at the mangled mess of what used to be James as he lay across the floor, no longer moving as his heads muscle pulsated with blood oozing onto the ground beneath him.

Candy Cane

Chapter Fifteen:

'Though we're apart, you're in my heart this holiday season...'

Hours fled past as the sunset turned into the darkness of night, the air bitter as the sky shed white tears; gracing the floor with the icy flow of snow. The Millers house lit up through the curtains as the lights gave off a safe, warm feeling of Christmas joy; but if you had ventured inside, you'd see hell itself. Bodily fluids sept into the carpet giving the house a horrid stench, as blood mixed with bile and stomach acid created a strange dark red- almost brown puddle underneath the Christmas tree, as if it was the trees skirt.

Organs still dripped their juices down the fake tree branches, a body filled mortifying Christmas tree. Eyes hung from it like clouded baubles as a child's head rested in the middle of it, his head scalped of any hair as his tongue hung just beside him; attached to the tree

Candy Cane

with twine. His once emerald green eyes were now clouded and used as decoration for the horrifying tree. His left mutilated leg was strung up by twine across the fireplace as it dripped onto the stoned floor below. It was just like a stocking ready for Santa's arrival, or should we say *Krampus*?

The kitchen table was stained with deep marks as the hatchet sat embedded into it, crimson red dripping off it as the stove blared behind it. A dusted old iron pot boiled over as the water overflowed almost spitting the fire out. Two pristine ivory white plates sat on the counter where the broken whisky glass still lay, rather than the four from that morning. Two still lay on the floor completely shattered and coated in the sticky redness. William hummed a darkened Christmas tune of *'Here comes Santa Claus'* as he drifted around the butcher like kitchen, blood staining every surface, alongside cutlery as he placed food upon the plates; steaming broccoli with mash and a concoction of meats being brought out from the boiling pot. Pork mixed

Candy Cane

with human thigh, boiled and then thrown into the oven to cook and give it a crunchy texture. The gravy he made was thick with added blood from the mason jar that he had collected from James's scalped head an hour prior.

"Dinner is almost ready my little dove, look outside, it is snowing!" William shouted towards the stairs as he heard slight movement through the thin floorboards. His grin widened more as he poured the gravy mixed with blood over the dinner that he had made for them both.

Grabbing a small plastic pastel pink cup, he filled it with cold water as he picked the scorching hot place up with his bare hand, not feeling the intense heat coming off it as his other hand held the cup and silver cutlery. Heading towards the stairs, they sang their creaking melody with each step he took. Reaching the top of the staircase, the creaking stopped as the small whimpers came from behind the ivory white door with blue butterflies illustrated across it. Smiling gently, William

Candy Cane

approached the door with caution as he bent down, setting the food down just for a moment as he pulled out a small delicate key; slowly entering it into the tiny hole as he turned it slightly to the left as it '*clicked*' softly.

"My little turtledove, I have dinner and a drink for you..." William cooed as he pushed the door slightly with his elbow, before bending down to grab hold of her food again.

Sidney's room was pastel pink with white stripes around it as blue butterflies cascaded down the walls. The dolls house sat in the far-right corner near the window next to her white bookcase, littered with her favourite fairytales from Cinderella to Rapunzel. A small table sat in the middle of the room where Sidney used to host her little tea parties with her teddies and dolls, but her favourite guest was always having her father come in and join in on her imaginary dramas between her Brittney Dolls arguing with her teddies. Finally, her

Candy Cane

pink metal bed frame sat in the far-right corner, a canopy of pink tulle covered across her bed as if she was a princess.

"Come on over darling, before your food gets too cold." William smiled as he placed her food down onto her table alongside her water as he knelt next to it, his arms on his legs, still stained in blood as he watched his daughter's body move from the darkness of her bed.

"D... daddy, my h... head hurts." Her voice whimpered as she slowly moved towards the light, holding onto her stuffed giraffe she had since she was a baby. She took him everywhere, naming him 'Gaff' because she had trouble saying '*Giraffe*' and William never had the heart to correct her; so 'Gaff' it was.

"I know my dove, but he's gone now. No one will *ever* hurt you again." William cooed as his voice growled softly as he remembered what that brute did to her, then satisfaction falling upon him knowing he could never hurt anyone again.

Candy Cane

Slowly shuffling towards the bottom of the bed, Sidney's eyes burned from the light hitting them; a side effect from the concussion she had succumb to earlier. As her little frail frame came into the light, her hair hung on by a couple strands of skin as William did his best to wrap her wounded head with a now blood-soaked bandage. Her trembling little body sat in her fluffy pink and white hearted Polka dot pyjamas as she clung onto Gaff as if her life depended on it. Tears pricked her wide blue eyes as the pain began again, scorching through her head and traveling into her eyes as she shut them tightly; like an intense migraine. Whimpers escaped through her shivering body as she hugged Gaff harder, William's expression growing darker as he saw her in so much pain; his own daughter in that much pain and he couldn't do anything to help her.

"My little turtledove it's okay, Daddy's coming." William softly spoke as he shuffled towards her wrapping his blood encrusted arms around her, pulling her in and

Candy Cane

shielding her from the harsh light as her tears fell onto his shirt.

"Daddy will make sure you're always safe my dove. Have some food when you can, I just need to go and get you some medicine to make the headaches stop. Okay?" He whispered as he felt his daughters head nod slowly, more tears falling into his shirt as he lifted her gently and placed her back onto the bed. Covering her up in her butterfly bedding, he walked towards the door and switched the light off quickly, watching the dim light turn the room into complete darkness. All he could hear was the faint drops of snow on her window and Sidney's whimpers of pain.

"I'll be back soon my dove, try to have a bit of food whilst I'm gone, please." William asked in a whisper as he pulled the door to softly, trying not to make it squeak too loud.

"Th… thank you Daddy, I love you." Sidney stuttered as her little body shifted in the darkness. William sighed as

Candy Cane

he closed the door, locking it again with the small key placing it back in his pocket.

Rushing next door to his room, William placed his worn-out black boots on as he dug once again through his wardrobe until he found his red long jacket, that had unfortunately lost a battle with some moths as it relished some holes around it; holding his keys tight and heading to the front door.

Candy Cane

Chapter Sixteen:

'Fairy Lights on Winter Nights...'

As the front door clicked softly shut, the snow had fallen quick and thick. The ground was a wasteland of innocent white as the droplets of water had iced over, encasing them in a beautiful imagery; freezing them forever in the last place they were. As the winter air blew minus degree wind, William walked towards his dusted old truck and clambered in. His eyes lay upon the blood stained seat beside him where Sidney was hours prior, and anger shot through him again.

"I'm so glad that fucker is gone." He mumbled as he turned the engine over. The truck spit and roared as the headlights flickered through the thick falling snow.

As the truck slowly reversed, a horned like shadow appeared in front of it. Holding the book in hand as the voice whispered its way through the broken radio, a sinister deep voice filled the cars speakers as William sat

Candy Cane

frozen, as if in a trance. Listening closely, his hands gripped the cold steering wheel through his white gloves.

"Continue the ritual... It's almost time... His time... So many naughty people who need to be punished..."

His blood ran cold as his hair stood on end under his coat. The shadowed figure came close to the wing mirror, until it vanished in the blink of an eye as the book lay opened on the bonnet of his truck. The snow barely glided off the pages as they illustrated a beast looking creature; holding a sack with chains around his hooves, his yellow eyes radiating in the winter's night sky. Captivating William to step out of his broken truck, he watched as the pages flipped through the cold breeze; showing him what he must do in order to let *him* out. Placing his frost bitten hands around the skin like book, William took it to the truck resting it on his dashboard as he opened his garage door, an array of tools scattered across the floor as he picked up ice

Candy Cane

picks, snow chains for his wheels, an axe, his small red tool box and a blow torch. Placing them all in the back of the truck, he eventually got back in and gently drove down the snow covered road.

"The Krampusnacht is coming and so am I..." William growled deep as he glanced at himself in the rear view mirror, his eyes were engulfed in yellow; glimmering under the street-lamps as he passed them by. His nails ripped through the ends of his gloves as he grinned wide, smelling the naughty ones as he drove down the iced road.

Travelling through the sleeping town, the trucks overworked engine was the only thing you could hear as a few shops still had the odd customer staggering out their doors, and into the freezing temperatures of the snowy night. With their brown paper bags moistened by the falling snow, a liquor bottle shimmered through the slowly ripping bag. On other side of the road were young adults staggering out of bars or clubs, as the

Candy Cane

bright neon lights suddenly switched off showing a bright yellow- ish dimmed light. Security guards patrolled the doors, watching as young girls walked into the freezing weather with hardly anything on as their skirts rose up.

"Idiots..." William scoffed as he pulled into his nearest open 24-hour corner shop, climbing back out of the warm truck and into the snowy ground. The gravel under his boots crunched softly as he headed towards the door.

Pushing the illuminated glass door with ease, the small bell jingled inside. William smiled weakly as he nodded towards the clearly exhausted teenage boy behind the counter, whose face looked as if it was a pepperoni pizza; all greasy and covered in pimples that were ready to burst. His snow-covered shoes squeaked slightly as he walked across the laminated flooring, heading towards the isle called *First Aid and Home Wear.*' As his tired eyes scanned the shelves, he held onto three

Candy Cane

packs of bandages as he reached for *'Calpol'* and a pack of *'Paracetamol.'* He placed both tablet packs into his arms with the bandages and walked around the miniature corner shop, browsing as he looked at chocolate; not for him, but for his daughter. When he saw up by the counter that there was a deal on for *'Candy Canes- pack of thirty of $20.'* Not wasting a moment, William snatched them up with his spare hand, placing them all down onto the counter as he smiled widely.

"What a great deal, my daughter loves Candy Canes!" He chirped as he pushed the pile of medical equipment and peppermint treats towards the cashier, who looked as if he'd rather be anywhere other than there.

"Cool dude, that'll be $32.98 please, cash or card?" The cashier spoke, his voice in-between the stages of puberty as his pitch sank between high and low, almost sounding like a certain cartoon mouse.

Candy Cane

"Card please, thank you." William replied as he pulled out his wife's card from his wallet. 'Might as well use the money she had left in her account. She's not going to use it.' He thought to himself, chuckling slightly at the thought as the '*beep*' of the card accepting the money snapped him out of his deep thoughts.

"Here you go, Merry Christmas or whatever." The young boy said as he turned back to his phone, pushing the plastic bag towards William.

"Thank you, you too buddy." He replied, taking the bag as he walked towards the door as it gave that darling little jingle when he pulled it open, letting the cold breeze in again.

Turning his head towards his truck, something felt off. Looking around the now blizzard snowstorm of the parking lot, a shadowy figure stood by the driver's side of the truck; his stare not wavering as he stepped closer to the figure who he could see. The figure was now trying to get into his truck, holding a crowbar as they

Candy Cane

pushed it into the gap between the door, pushing on it desperately trying to get it open.

"Come on you pile of shit! Move!" The figure grunted as he pushed harder, his feet slipping from under him as the snow made the floor extremely slippery.

William caught his reflexion in the side mirror as he approached the thief, his eyes completely yellow and glowing like stars in the midnight sky, as he stood behind the man trying to break into his truck.

"Can I help you, sir?" William's voice growled as the bells started their murderous hum once again, and he gripped the plastic bag hard.

Candy Cane

Chapter Seventeen:

'The spirit of giving...'

The thief's head snapped around as quickly as if he was possessed, as his hands still stayed frozen on his crowbar that was wedged into the truck. Snow fell faster as the ground was now an icy winter wonderland. William's face stayed cold as his eyes fixated on the man in front of him, glowing deep yellow through the white droplets.

"Do I have to ask again? Because I really don't want to..." William sneered as his eyes glowed brighter, his frustration getting the better of him as he gripped the plastic bag harder.

"N.. No sir, I... erm..." The thief stuttered as his body shook, either due to the freezing air or the fear of being caught.

Candy Cane

Staring intensely, William noticed something about the trembling man in front of him. He was also in the waiting room that day of the interview. His round belly and short facial hair alongside the pig snout for a nose, and glistening blue eyes sparked his memory as he smiled slightly. The bells murderous jingle continued in the back of his mind like a nagging headache that wouldn't leave as he stepped a little closer to the man.

"You were at the mall, weren't you? For the Santa Claus position?" William sighed as he watched his prey writhe under his gaze. The thief trembled, still latching onto the crowbar as if it was life or death.

"How did you...?" The thief started to question before he tilted his head to the side, taking a longer look at William before the penny dropped. "You're the crazy bastard they had dragged out of there!" His eyes widened as he stared at him, realisation hitting him hard.

Candy Cane

"Well, I wouldn't have put it that way, but yeah-that manager was up her own arse." William scowled as he remembered the terrible encounter in Susan Jone's office, his eyes phantom stinging from the hand sanitiser being thrown into them.

"Yet you were the one who got dragged out of her office screaming like a druggie?" The man scoffed as he sniffled slightly, the slimy green snot that had dripped from his nose frozen in place from the icy winds.

"What was your name again? I don't recall that you told me- since you're trying to break into my truck." William growled softly as he set the plastic bag down by his feet, giving his clenched knuckles a rest.

"It's... ermm... it's none of your fucking business pal." The thief shouted as his grip grew tighter on the crowbar, gathering the strength to pull it from the door.

"I wouldn't do that; it won't end well for you!" William warned as he stepped a hair closer to the thief, his eyes

Candy Cane

glowing deep yellow through the snow as his hands cracked. His sharp talon like claws ripped through the gloves with ease.

"Yeah, right and what are you going to do? Claw at me like you did Susan?" The thief smirked as his trembling from the cold hands tugged against the icy crowbar, feeling its full weight release from the truck and landing to his left side with a soft *'thud.'*

"You won't live to see another Christmas, so I'll ask one last time! What is your name and why do you want to get in my truck so badly?" William sneered as he watched the crowbar fall to the man's side, the bells thundering their murderous orchestra; getting louder with each snowflake that fell.

"The ritual must be completed... The naughty must be punished..." Whispered the sinister voice as it slithered into William's head through the bells, as he growled low like a lion warning its prey. His claw were like talons

Candy Cane

that crunched and clicked as the winter wind blew harder.

"Fuck you! You creepy bastard, I'm not going to tell you my name!" The thief shouted as he raised the heavy iron crowbar above his head, holding it with both shaking arms as he drove it towards William's face; the wind whistling as the iron bar flew through the air.

Tilting his head to the side slightly, the thief waited to hear a crack from where the bar connected to William's face, but nothing came; no whimpering from pain, no shouting from anger. Nothing. Confused by the silence, the thief turned his head back to see that the crowbar was still by William's face, however, his white ripped glove was wrapped around the icy bar like white and black snakes as he smirked; his eyes bellowing yellow as if fire was roaring out of them. Pulling with an inhumane amount of strength, William gripped the bar; bringing it towards him as the thief followed behind it. For a scrawny man, it baffled the thief and knocked him

Candy Cane

off his guard. Grinning like the cheshire cat, William pulled the thief to his face as his eyes were two balls of yellow raging fires watching him intensely. In one swift motion, William twisted the crowbar to the left, in an unnatural way as the thief's arm snapped as easy as a twig; his humerus bone breaking through his skin. Becoming an open wounded fracture, his fresh red blood stained the innocent purity of the white snow, making him drop the crowbar instantly. The thief's screams of agony were drowned out quickly as William clenched his fist and landed a blow on his nose, not enough effort to kill him, but enough to knock him unconscious as his body crumbled to the snowy ground. His blood created a deadly pool in the innocence below him.

"I told you so, fucking dickhead!" William roared as his head tilted forward, watching as the thief's chest still moved, indicating that he was still alive; despite the trauma of his arm being snapped.

Candy Cane

Reaching down, William grasped the crowbar. Throwing it into the back of his truck, he turned to his shopping bag. Unlocking the car door, he placed the bag on the back seat as he watched the thief, his head tilting to the side like a dog trying to understand something. That was when he heard a buzzing come from inside of his pocket. Standing over the snow infested with the thief's blood, William reached into the man's pocket, grabbing his phone as he pulled it up. The screen almost burned his eyes as the harsh light invaded them, and an array of text messages appeared on the screen. Once William's eyes adjusted to the sudden lightness, it read;

- _Susan Jones:_ Have you got the job done yet?
- _Susan Jones:_ Hello? Did you find anything?
- _Susan Jones:_ GREG ANSWER ME! Did you find anything on that creepy son of a bitch?
- _Susan Jones:_ GREG! IF YOU DO NOT ANSWER KISS YOUR JOLLY JOB GOODBYE THIS YEAR! I HAVE PLENTY OF PEOPLE READY TO BE SANTA...

Candy Cane

"So, she hired you for my job, and then to spy on me? That heartless bitch! She'll have her turn soon. As for you..." William shouted as his anger grew just as quick and cold as the winter wind, his attention turning back to the mutilated man quivering underneath him.

Leaning down to the man's body, the intoxicating smell of coppery blood ventured into his nose. His stomach growled wildly as William remembered he hadn't eaten at all that day. Bending his head towards the sticky puddle of cooling blood, his instincts kicked in as he lapped it up like a starving beast. Lifting his head up, his lower jaw dripped red liquid; his eyes locked onto his meal.

Candy Cane

Chapter Eighteen:

'All is calm, all is bright...'

Dragging Greg's body though the thickening snow by his ankles, a smear of blood from his mutilated arm was all that was left behind as William hoisted his still passed out body into his backseat. Blood gathered into the bottom floor of his truck as William started his rumbling engine again. Backing out of the white covered parking lot, rage fuelled him as his hands shook uncontrollably; the coppery taste still lingering on his tongue as his face stained the redness of the liquid he had just tasted.

"*Don't trust anyone William... continue the ritual... Correct the mistakes done by the wrong themselves... Make them pay...*" The sinister voice whispered through the static radio as his anger bubbled and boiled. Susan only had a taste of what he could do, but now with his strength... now, she would suffer for the pain she had caused, and for what she had done to him. Snow

Candy Cane

glistened like white diamonds across the covered streets under his flickering headlights, sparkling like icy crystals falling from the sky.

The overwhelming stench of copper lingered in the truck from Greg's still bleeding arm. William's stomach ached and roared with hunger, the sample he had earlier of the liquid only made him more ravenous. Glancing towards the plastic store bought bag, the sweet smell of the minty peppermint wafted through the slightly opened bag; it must have popped when he placed it from the floor to the truck. Reaching down with his once white and now spotted red gloved claw, he reached into the bag for one of the striped candy canes; pulling out the hooked object as he ripped the seal off with this teeth, eager to get into the minty treat.

Placing the bottom of the minty stick into his mouth, William sucked and played with it in his mouth—savouring the peppermint taste. Due to his wife's strong beliefs of Christmas just being a holiday the government

Candy Cane

made to bring in more money, he never truly had the chance to enjoy a candy cane. Chuckling to himself he realised that for the first time in years he was allowed to have what he wanted with no consequences... As long as he abided by the rules of the book.

Glazing out the frosted window, with the red and white striped cane still hanging from his mouth, William noticed a sign hanging by the entrance of the forest park. *'Closed for repairs. Do Not Enter.'* An idea sparked in his clouded mind as he turned the truck, taking a sharp left towards the park. Grinning wildly, he pulled up into the untouched parking lot. Snow coated the entire parking lot like a soft white blanket, glistening under the moonlight as the cold air frosted over everything it touched. The air was bitterly cold as William opened the door slightly; the cold turning the tip of his nose red as he kept the minty stick in his mouth, trying to fight off the hunger he felt. Turning his attention to his hostage that was still bleeding from his wounded arm, William hoisted him over his shoulder as

Candy Cane

he placed his body down onto the innocent snowy floor. Turning to the back of the truck, he retrieved his chains as he wrapped them around Greg tightly and proceeded to drag his bound up body through the snow, towards the darkened forest ahead of him.

"Just a little further..." William said between slurps of his dampened mouth around the candy cane, his hunger still raging inside of him.

After walking half a mile as the snow thickened, William stopped under a tree arch as he propped Greg up against it, watching him as he scrolled down the conversation between him and Susan. As he did, his blood simmered, on the edge of over-boil as his anger spiked once again. His eyes fixated on the phone screen as he saw the two of them laughing behind his back, until he swiped off and saw a name that he never thought he'd see.

'Tilly Miller' with curiosity getting the better of him, he clicked his dead wife's name. He immediately wished

Candy Cane

that he hadn't, as years' worth of deception and lies invaded his mind. Every time Tilly had said she was 'running late' or had to 'stay late' after school for their activities, she was actually living a double life. There were pictures of them on dates together, dancing, kissing to even sleeping in the bed he bought. The most heart aching thing was seeing the man with his arm around Sidney, holding her as his own daughter. But the slap in the face came when William noticed Greg's features- dark black hair like a crows feather, to his shimmering emerald green eyes; just like James had. The years of betrayal from them had his entire body shaking, his eyes illuminating with deep yellow as they engulfed the dull blue. His body snapped and crunched as he let out an animalistic growl, so loud it made the crows in the trees above suddenly flee. The dull red coat ripped in areas as his body shifted, more hunched over as Williams arms grew slightly longer; his hands showing no skin as they were covered by a dark brown fur. Talons sharp as glass pointed at the end of the

Candy Cane

ripped gloves, and he wasn't William anymore. He was the embodiment of what was to come, and he was here to correct the cosmic mistakes made by those who didn't believe. But now they would.

"We told you the truth... Let your anger out... it is time William..." The sinister voice whispered, blowing through the freezing breeze that made the trees shake slightly.

Greg groaned as his head started to lift slightly, his eyes bloodshot from the pain as his vision was blurred; and all he could make out was a darkened figure stood by him.

Candy Cane

Chapter Nineteen:

'Peace on Earth...'

Shaking his head slightly, the pain came rushing back as Greg groaned. His head pounded as a headache came on quickly, and his vision came back after blinking a couple of times. His face dropped with terror as he tried to run, but he quickly found out that his body was strapped tightly up with the chains. Tears pricked the corners of his eyes as he watched the figure approach him slowly, the red and white hooked cane still hanging from William's mouth as he inched closer; with the phone still in hand.

"You were fucking my wife?" William asked, his voice deep and distorted as he wrapped one of his claws around the end of the candy canes frozen hook, pulling it to the right side.

Swallowing what little saliva he had left hard, Greg's mouth suddenly went as dry as sandpaper as panic

Candy Cane

arose in his body, his complexion turning pale as his cheeks flushed with a deep pink. His emerald eyes darted back and forth as sweat formed on his forehead, the below minus temperatures freezing it in place. His chest rose quickly as his hot breathe shot a cloud of grey from him breathing quickly, and he noticed his phone that was clutched in William's right claw.

"Hey Siri! Call the..." Greg shouted with his hoarse voice as he saw the screen on his phone light up for a moment; although it was only for that moment. William's claws grasped around the frosted screen, gripping it hard and scratching it; before it cracked, and finally snapped. Greg's face fell in defeat as his spirit of getting help shattered, just like his phone had as the broken device fell to the ground; landing into the snowy bed with a soft *'thud.'*

"You didn't answer me. So much for my evidence of the whore my wife is... well was." William snickered as

Candy Cane

he wiped the fibreglass from his claw, stepping towards Gregs shivering body.

Whimpering Greg closed his eyes as fear took control of his body, his only way of help was now cracked on the snow fallen ground. His heart stopped for a second as he heard William correct himself, *'what happened to Tilly? Is that why she wasn't at school pick up or wasn't answering my calls?'* he thought to himself as the frost bit at his exposed skin.

"What do you mean *'was?'* Where is Tilly? Where are the children?" Greg barked as fear writhed in his voice. He needed to know if they were okay. He needed to know if his **son** was okay.

"How dare you ask about my daughter, she would've been fine if your brat of a son didn't scalp her, and cause her to have a concussion!" William growled as his anger exploded. Suddenly, he ran forward towards Greg, forcing him as far back as he could go and into the tree. Without warning, the arch of his back was

Candy Cane

prodded from behind by a rogue and frozen sharp branch.

"What are you fucking on about? My son? James is yours?" Greg whimpered back still trying to live out the ridiculous lie. He thought maybe if he could make William believe that James was his, he could be freed; but in doing so, he sealed his own fate.

"Liar." William spat. With hatred filling his body, he withdrew the candy cane from his mouth as s string of saliva dangled from the red and white stick, and the end had been sucked down to a sharp point. Within seconds of the warm saliva riddled stick being in the cold air, it was frozen to the deadly point that even the droplets of saliva froze to it as well. Greg froze in fear as his body stiffened. He didn't dare move as William crouched down on all fours, crawling towards Greg like a beast ready to pounce. Holding the deadly stick as the end shimmered under the moonlight, William's eyes illuminated like cats under a torch as they seemed to

Candy Cane

glow out of their sockets. The closer that he came to Greg the more fear he felt in his body as he tried to wiggle out of his chains, but he had no hope.

Sitting over Greg, William's body seemed heavier as he saw the fur peeking out from under his clothes. The overwhelming mixed smell of decay and peppermint filled Greg's sinuses as William's body bent forward, giving a loud '*crack*' as his spine deformed. His hot breath left goosebumps on Greg's neck as he leaned into his ear, and he could feel the strange creature's lips turning into a smile as William's mouth opened one last time.

"Say hi to that whore of a wife for me- and your darling little shit of a son..." William whispered, growling low as his voice dissipated into a demonic pitch; the wind blowing harder as the sounds of ancient bells jingled their murderous melody.

The sound of cloven hooves danced around them in the snow as William raised the deadly candy cane in the air

Candy Cane

as he dug it into Greg's neck. Wasting no time, he drove it deeper and across his neck as it split in two; severing his vocal cords and muscle with such force you could see the white bone of his spine peeking through. His neck exploded with a river of red, cascading down his body like the red sea in Egypt.

They always said that the river Nile was a river in Egypt, and Greg had gone to it permanently as his face froze in his last moments of his life; terror. Pulling the blood-soaked candy cane from deep within his neck, William placed it in his mouth as he sucked every bit of blood off it; letting the mixture of copper and mint dance in his mouth before he snapped the bottom of it off, spitting it at Greg where it landed in his open neck wound.

"One more down... You are close to finishing the ritual William... Set him free..." The wind blew the sinister voice around him as his hunger gave way. Taking control of his actions, he lunged down as he bit into

Candy Cane

Greg's neck; the cold frost-bitten pieces of skin and muscle ripping away.

Chewing quickly and swallowing, William devoured his dead wife's secret lover. As he swallowed, he took the candy canes jagged edge, cutting a messy circle around Greg's face and lifting a corner as he pulled it gently. He could feel the flappy skin tear away from the face muscle, his eyelids and lips being the only things left behind as he placed the skinned mask face down and onto the blood soaked snowy floor; so the blood could freeze over. Stabbing what was left of the candy cane into the snow, William stood back admiring what he had done, and he glanced back to the broken phone. Picking it up alongside the frozen skinned face, he placed them into his pocket as he walked back to the truck; leaving behind deep bloody footprints in the innocent snow. Walking half a mile back, his body didn't change. It didn't return to normal, his claws didn't retract and he was stuck with fur and claws; and yet he didn't care. Stuck in the monstrous form he was

Candy Cane

destined, he knew it was because he was the chosen one. The one who would set Krampus free, the one who make the world fear him once again; and if they didn't, they would be punished.

Gripping his truck door, William pulled it slightly as he stepped inside, sitting behind the wheel as he placed the broken phone and skinned face of Greg on the dashboard. Reaching for his own phone, William had an idea. Using his claw to get his SIM card out, he swapped it with Gregs and watched as the messages came flooding through. Since Gregs phone was damaged completely, his SIM card was the key to getting Susan in his grasps, all without drawing too much attention.

Candy Cane

Chapter Twenty:

'Have Yourself a Merry Little Christmas…'

Grinning wide, his clawed fingers typed viciously against his phone as he opened the messages regarding Susan, his heart pounding hard against his chest with excitement as he messaged her:

- *Gregory Smith:* All done. Come meet me at Forest Park, I have everything that you wanted, and more…

His eyes glued onto the screen as he saw the text bubble with three dots appear at the bottom left of the corner. The anticipation made his anger simmer as he waited for her reply. Leaning down he placed three more candy cane sticks into his pocket as he jumped hearing the phone familiar '*ping.*'

- *Susan Jones:* About time you fucking messaged back, I'll be there in five minutes, need to make

Candy Cane

sure Teddy is asleep. I thought you fucked off with Tilly again, can't trust the pair of you together!

"She knew... She fucking knew they were together and that's why she wouldn't hire me!" William growled low as his teeth ground together, his anger on the point of over-boiling. William scrolled up through more of their conversation, reading that Susan would decline William the job and give it to Greg, and how it would benefit Greg and Tilly spending more time together.

Turning his engine off, his headlights died out. William sat waiting in his car as five minutes passed, with no sign of her still. His anger brewed as he reached for the phone once again, checking to see if she had messaged; but she hadn't. Opening their conversation once more, William typed back to her:

- *Gregory Smith:* Where are you? I think he saw me... Hurry!

Candy Cane

Discarding the phone back to the passenger's seat, William rested his head on his hands, gripping the steering wheel as he closed his eyes momentarily. He was thinking of a way to get hold of Susan without being caught. No sound came from the phone as he sighed, reaching for the key to turn the engine back on as it roared back alive. Backing out of the snowy parking lot, the phone '*pinged*' again. Excitement and anger mixed as William reached over with his right hand, turning the device on as his excitement fizzled away to pure annoyance as he read her message.

- <u>Susan Jones:</u> Can't get away tonight, Teddy needs me. Speak to you at work tomorrow, meet in my office.

Sighing, he pulled over to the right as he replied to her as quickly as he could without sounding too suspicious:

- <u>Gregory Smith:</u> Ok, will do. See you tomorrow!

Throwing the phone back down to the passenger's side, William growled as he spun the truck around heading

Candy Cane

back home to Sidney as he mumbled to himself, his anger almost causing him to knock over a drunken man who stumbled into the road. The snow icicles pinged off the fast-moving vehicle like bullets as William pulled into his driveway. Gripping the plastic bag, he sighed hard as he slammed the car door, as the bang echoed through the wind. Walking slowly, blood still covered the bottom of his boots and William pushed the key into the door as he stumbled inside as if he had just come home from a night on the town.

"Honey, I'm home." He chuckled as he locked the door behind him, heading towards the stairs as they creaked louder under his new weight.

Reaching the top of the stairs, the floorboards sounded as if they we're going to cave in as he reached into his pocket, pulling out the small and slender key to Sidney's room. He opened the door, pushing it gently as he entered the dark room.

Candy Cane

"Sid, sweetie- I have stuff for you." He cooed as he looked around the dark room, seeing her little body move slightly in her bed. He smiled softly as he looked over to her plate, seeing that she had eaten some of the mixed meat alongside emptying her drinking cup.

Placing two candy canes on her table, he picked up her half-eaten dinner with her cup as he walked back into his room; throwing the plastic bag and plate to the ground as the food smeared across the wall and floor. Walking into the bathroom with her cup, he placed it under the cold tap as he turned it on. As he did, he looked up into the mirror; staring as his own reflection for the first time that night. His eyes were sunken in almost like two blackened holes and his face was droopy, with his cheek bones poking through the paper-thin skin. His reflection made his memory revert to the nightmare as he remembered what the old woman was like- how her face was sunken in, just like his. The cold water splashing on his hand snapped him out of his trance as he picked up the cup, rushing out

Candy Cane

of the bathroom and back into his room. He rummaged around in the plastic bag before picking up the paracetamol packet and then finally walked back into Sidney's room.

Placing the water down on her desk next to the candy canes, he popped one paracetamol tablet out as the chalk like tablet connected to the plastic table. He shuffled towards his daughters sleeping body as he saw her head had leaked blood and mucus into her pillow, her little arms wrapped round her giraffe as her face seemed peaceful. He placed a kiss on her forehead as her eyelids fluttered open just for a moment as she smiled weakly at him.

"Daddy, you're home!" Her tired little voice croaked as she wiped the sleep from her left eye.

"Go back to sleep my angel. I have to go to work early tomorrow, but thank you for eating something." He smiled as he replied, kissing her head softly again and holding back a tear as the sight of her in pain hurt him the most.

"My head hurts, did you get any medicine?" Sidney whispered as she held her head with her left arm, wincing at the loud wind banging against the window.

"Yes, my turtle dove. I've placed a tablet on the table for you. Only take it when the pain is too much, I'll be home late tomorrow, so I'll slide the key to your door under it, okay? Now go back to sleep my angel. I love you." William cooed as he kissed her one last time, standing up as he walked towards the door and closed it gently; as he locked it.

Struggling to get to his own bed as exhaustion hit him hard, William's body collapsed on the floor of his room as the lights went dark. In a deep sleep, he forgot to set his alarm. As he turned over, he whacked his head hard against his bed frame; waking him up in a panic as he looked over to his clock seeing that it read, **10:00am**. Frantically checking his phone, William saw he had

Candy Cane

three missed texts and one missed call from Susan that read:

- *Susan Jones:* I'm at work, where are you?
- *Susan Jones:* Greg where are you? You're five minutes late?
- *Susan Jones:* If you at not in this mall by 11:00am I am going to make sure you're not breathing once I get my hands on you! Stop getting your dick wet with Tilly and GET TO WORK!

Growling low at the last message, William stormed out of his bedroom and towards the stairs as he ran down them. The creaking of the stairs felt like a distant hum to him as he walked towards the front door. Slamming it hard behind him, William got in his truck and sped off towards the mall, completely forgetting to put Sidney's key under her door.

"I'll make sure you're not fucking breathing." William mumbled as he gripped the steering wheel harder,

Candy Cane

running through three red lights as he parked up outside the mall. Flipping down his visor, he grabbed Greg's skinned face as he positioned it over his own as he rummaged around trying to find a hat of some sort, before finding his old rotten, moth-eaten beanie.

Walking with his head hung low, William made his way through the busy mall as parents shifted through massive crowds of people doing their annual Christmas shop. The carols blasted through the rusted old speakers, repeating the same songs as he spotted Santa's Grotto in the far back corner; and his speed picked up. Finally getting to the Grotto, an elf about five-foot four stood checking a clipboard as a line of fussy children were already stood waiting to meet the big man himself.

"Hey... ermm I'm Greg. I'm a bit late, Where should I go?" William spoke as he lowered his voice to imitate the man's voice; who's face he was wearing as a Halloween mask.

Candy Cane

"Ugh so you're Greg? Go around the back of the Grotto, your suit should be in there!" The elf said as her voice sounded fed up already. She didn't look up from her clipboard, she just pointed behind her to the Grotto.

A nodding William shuffled towards the back of the Grotto as he walked into the staff room. A red suit hung up, sparkling like he'd always imagined as he noticed a fake beard and hair with a bright red hat, with a white bobble at the end. Quickly changing out of his blood crusted clothes, William clambered into the jolly man's suit as he felt the velvet suit hug him tightly. The white facial hair hid where he had carved earlier around Greg's mouth as the hair hid the slits around the top of the face. Walking back out into the Grotto, the children gasped and cheered as William waved and walked to his velvet chair. He finally sat down as he waited for the children to come, to tell him him who had been naughty, or nice.

Candy Cane

Hours passed by as children of all ages came to sit on his lap. Every thirty minutes William stood and went to readjust his face, as the heat of the lights above him thawed the face from its frozen position; making it droop. Susan passed by the Grotto a couple times as he caught a glimpse of her in the corner of his eye, but couldn't do anything about it.

"Santa..." A young girl the same age as his daughter hobbled up out of her wheelchair, her chestnut brown hair parted in two small pigtails as her large brown eyes stared at him in awe.

"Yes child, what can I do for you?" William smiled as he lifted her onto his lap, and she coughed slightly at the sudden movement before looking into his eyes; her eyes slightly watery.

"F... for Christmas I just want my mommy and daddy back. We got into an accident on the road, and they never woke up again. I live with my aunty now, but I'd really like them back please. I've been really good this

Candy Cane

year, I promise." Her voice was as soft as a whisper as a small tear dropped down her face. Swallowing hard, William looked behind her to see a woman that was stood talking to the elf, as he turned back to her sighing.

"My darling I can't bring your parents back. I'm sorry. But remember they love you, and will always be with you- in here." William pointed to her chest where her heart was. "Just because you can't see them doesn't mean they are not there, trust me- I know." William winked as she giggled slightly. "Take this with you and remember to always be good. I'm always watching, but if you're naughty, my brother Krampus will come and get you." William smiled as he passed her a pristinely wrapped candy cane. As she took it, she thanked him and headed back to her wheelchair.

Candy Cane

Chapter Twenty-One:

'Hope Your Christmas Is Perfect...'

Leaning over to his side, he placed the sign down on the chair as he walked towards the elf for the final time, nodding as he walked towards the manager's office; his face barely staying on as he wandered down the hallway. He knew all too well as the memory of being dragged away from it spited him. As he raised his fist and knocked three times on the door, he saw a light flicker on inside as he heard Susan's grating voice reply to him.

"For god's sake, Come in! The door is open." She sounded frustrated already.

With a shaking hand, William reached for the silver handle as he pushed it down and opened it, stepping inside the door before it swung close again; making her jump this time instead of him. Her little gasp she made from fear of the door made him excited to hear what

Candy Cane

her screams would soon sound like. Grinning William turned on his heels to face her as she stared at him, her frustration painted clear on her face.

"Why the fuck were you late today, Greg? I gave you this job because I knew you'd be reliable! If you want me to keep my trap shut about you, Tilly and the little devil spawn of yours, you really should do as I say!" Susan coldly stated as her makeup caked face frowned, her hair straightened as it cascaded down her shoulders and back. As she leaned forward on her chair, her painted acrylic nails interlocked with each other as she rested her head on them. Trying and failing to be intimidating, she looked William up and down with disgust.

"Why did you come into my office dressed like that Twat?" Susan questioned as she spat at him. Her hatred for the holiday was almost as bad as Tilly's, which only fuelled William as the bells grew louder once more in his head.

Candy Cane

"Because I'm not Greg..." William mumbled as he stepped more into the light. The face he was wearing now drooped to one side looking as if he had a stroke.

Susans eyes widened as fear invaded her mind, frozen in place as she stared at the man in front of her. A sudden little breeze wafted in from under the doorframe as a small jingle of bells carried by the wind. Reaching up in one motion, William tore the face off his as it ripped from the amount of pressure he had put it through by constantly readjusting it. Disregarding Greg's face, William threw it on the desk in front of Susan as he watched her mouth open, although no sound came out as she stared at the ripped face of Greg's.

"G... Greg?" Susan whimpered as she put her hand out to touch his face.

"You knew..." William stared as he growled low, his eyes glowing yellow softly as he walked forward towards her.

Candy Cane

"You knew she was cheating on me, that James wasn't mine and yet you still said, 'like father like son.' Who's the monster now, SUSAN?" William growled loud as he launched over the table again, grabbing a handful of her hair slamming her face into the desk. Something shiny caught his eye as she wailed in pain, trying to use her acrylic nails to claw at his hand, but not having any luck.

A pen in the shape of a candy cane sat staring at him as he smiled wide, grabbing it with his free hand. As he ripped the bottom of it off with his teeth, he revealed the sharp inked end of it as he leaned down to see Susan's mascara stained face from her tears. He rested his chin on her neck laughing maliciously as the demonic pitch came through, making his voice distorted.

"P... please let me g... go! Th... think of Teddy!" Susan pleaded as she sniffled hard, feeling her extensions ripping from her head the more he pulled her back.

Candy Cane

"I am thinking Susan, and you know what?" William rhetorically asked as he put his mouth closer to her ear. The her hair on the back of her next stood up, making her almost piss herself with anxiety.

"I think he'd be better off without a snob of a mother like you. Give Tilly my love when you see her, you bitch." He whispered in her ear as he pushed the candy cane pen into her neck, twisting it as she gave an ear-piercing shriek. She waved her hand over the gash in her neck, but it was too late as her blood sprayed the room like a water sprinkler.

Bringing the pen higher again, William continued to stab her with it as small puncture wounds filled her dying body, until her head fell forward to the desk with a loud *'thump.'* No sound came from her anymore, not even a whimper as her body lay still with sticky red liquid dribbling onto the desk, as it dripped off the other side and onto the cold flooring. Sighing in relief, William walked to the other side of the desk as he

Candy Cane

collapsed onto the green chairs from before, still holding onto the blood covered pen. Closing his eyes he smiled as he heard nothing but the silent dripping of the blood falling from the desk to the floor.

"Excuse me? Susan, I heard you screaming and I..." The elf girl from before said as she opened the door, before giving a heart retching scream that made William jump in shock.

"It's not what it looks like!" William defended as he held his hands up, staring at her.

She shook her head and began running down the hallway, screaming as she almost tripped wearing the ridiculous curled shoes. William followed behind her, his animal instincts taking hold of him as the bells started again.

"*Kill her... Make her pay for her naughty sins... he's almost free...*" The sinister voice shouted in his head as he tackled her to the ground. She writhed underneath him trying to get free, but had no hope as he stabbed

Candy Cane

her repeatedly with the candy cane pen. He hadn't noticed that he was in the middle of the mall as families gathered around them.

After five minutes of hearing the wet slaps of the pen penetrate her skin, she moved no more as William finally looked up to see a crowd of people watching him, as children cried and multiple parents were on the phone to the police. He swallowed hard as he pushed through the crowd, running towards his truck as the outside world looked like a winter wonderland. In the distance, sirens wailed through the breeze as the red and blue lights came closer. William panicked as he turned to see the little girl from earlier that now looked at him in horror. Tears fell from his eyes as he opened his truck and sped past, the police who had just arrived to the scene; bursting through the doors and seeing the murdered elf girl that lay on the ground as they took statements from the onlookers.

Candy Cane

Speeding through multiple traffic lights, William made it home as he burst through the front door. Letting the cold air in, he ran up the creaking stairs towards Sidney's room, unlocking it quickly as he pushed the door to see her sat at her table with her Giraffe by her side; trying to cope with her head ache. Not realising he was covered completely in blood, he sat at the other end of her table as he reached his arms out to her.

"Daddy you're home! Did you spill ketchup down you again?" She giggled as her tiny hands took his.

"No darling listen, Daddy has to go away for a while okay. Nanar will come to look after you, but you must wait for the police to come. Do not leave this room, okay?" William's voice broke as tears filled his eyes once more, squeezing her hands as she whimpered slightly.

"What do you mean, daddy? Where are you going? Where are James and Mummy? I haven't heard them

Candy Cane

for a while." Sidney whimpered, worried slightly as her big blue eyes became watery.

"Just remember- I love you so much my turtle dove, okay? I need to go now, but do what I say, okay?" William sniffled as he pulled her closer, hugging his daughter one last time; placing her key on her table as he walked towards her door.

"I love you daddy, please don't go." Sidney cried after him as she sat holding her giraffe, squeezing him hard as she watched him walk out the door.

Crying hard as he closed her door one last time, William heard the sirens getting closer to their house as he ran into his room. Grabbing the bag of candy canes, he threw them into a backpack alongside some clothes and any money he had left, as he sprinted back down the stairs; just as a police car pulled up across from his truck.

Candy Cane

"This is where the prick lives right, Sarge?" He heard as one officer shouted to the other as he walked down his gravelled path.

Running towards the back door, William slipped through it as he hid behind the snow coated trash bins, keys in hand as he heard the Officers at his front door knocking loudly. Adrenaline seared through his veins as he watched their movements from around the corner. He was so close to getting away.

"Hello? Mr. Miller? We have permission to enter if you do not answer!" The Sergeant shouted as he nodded to the other as they both knocked the front door open, entering his house.

Taking his chance, William ran towards his truck as he opened it and jumped into the driver's seat, throwing the key in the ignition and turning it on as it roared to life. The Sergeant came running back out as he picked his walkie up, calling for back up to the house as he reported William's truck to them. The other officer

Candy Cane

stumbled into William's murder decorations as he screamed through the house, the body parts dangling from the tree that had attracted mice and flies and they embedded themselves into the mouth of Tilly; flying through her empty eye socket, and the same with James.

"Shit!" William mumbled as he drove through the city as sirens appeared in his rear-view mirror. He took a sharp left turn into the forest park, as he parked into his spot; jumping out of his truck and abandoning it as he ran towards the endless forest.

Three police cars parked up next to his truck as they followed swiftly after him. William was ahead for a while, before he heard a gunshot enclosing on him. Just a little closer to the edge and he could possibly hide. As he began running faster, his mind raced when suddenly a sharp pain soared through his stomach. Stopping for a second, he looked down, seeing blood that was

Candy Cane

oozing from a bullet wound as it spilled onto the floor below him.

"I got him! Stay right there, you sick fuck!" A police officer screamed as they ran up towards him. Still staggering, William saw the iced over lake as he stepped onto it as it held his weight barely.

With every step the ice creaked as he walked more into the middle, blood pooling out of the bullet wound that he had covered with his hand. The police had come closer, stepping onto the ice, fearing that if they got any closer to him- it would crack.

"Remember this as the reckoning, everyone who died was an instrument to the madness of society...." William shouted as he took a breath in. "Krampus chose me to become his resurrector and I have done that. Everyone who sees these murders will be feared by his work! Let the Krampusnacht begin!" William shouted as he stomped his foot. The ice instantly shattering beneath him as the icy water dragged him underneath. The

Candy Cane

police rushed to the hole, but it was too late- he had gone.

Back at the house Sidney had been escorted outside under a blanket as she held onto her Giraffe for dear life, tears streaming down her face as she saw a white Mercedes's pull up outside. Her grandparents Kristine and Albert had arrived to bring her with them, away from the murder house as the news reporters scattered around them. Albert walked forward with his short white hair and beard, thick black framed glasses and his dark blue, almost green eyes landed on his surviving granddaughter. As he knelt next to her, he held open his arms as he smiled gently towards her.

"Come on ducky, it's time to take you away from this mess." He smiled as he lifted her up in his arms. Her Nanar, Kristine slimmer with long white hair and a fringe smiled weakly with her blue ish green eyes watering as they strapped her into the car, taking her far away.

Candy Cane

As they drove out of the neighbourhood, Sidney looked back at the house that she had grown up in as the reporters and police surrounded the house. People were shouting and screaming, and as they got further away, her eyes released the last of her tears as she looked into the window of the kitchen; seeing a faded memory of her father on Christmas morning where they'd make breakfast together.

"Merry Christmas daddy, I love you." She whispered into her chair as she sat forward leaving them behind. The news pictured him as 'dangerous' and 'monster,' but Sidney only saw the good in him; because out of everyone in that house, he kept her alive.

Through every tradition, through every legend, a truth is hidden and for good reason. You better be good this year otherwise you won't just get coal. Krampus is out there and he's watching and waiting for you to be naughty. Will you end up in his book? In his list? Naughty or nice, we all pay the price. Have a Merry

Candy Cane

Christmas and a Happy New Year... if you make it that long.

Candy Cane

Authors Notes:

I hope you enjoyed your read of 'Candy Cane' and survived The Krampusnacht. I'd like to thank you my readers for your constant support, without you I wouldn't be able to live my dream and be who I am today. I'd like to give an extra special thank you to my Grandad, my Pappie, John Tilstone. Since my father passed away, he's stepped in and not only filled his shoes, but guided me through my strange life. He's done so much more than any Grandad, or Pappie should have, and I will forever be grateful for him. As this book is set to be released on his birthday, 10th December, I hope he knows just how loved he is and that he has a magical day. I hope whenever you see this book, it reminds you of how much we love and adore you. Happy Birthday Pappie, I love you hundreds!

Candy Cane

About the Author:

Katye Tilstone is a 23-year-old woman from the UK, her main interests consist of Horror Films, Monster High and Disney. She has a fiancé whom she adores and a loving family. Her black cat is called *'Lucifer'* who she loves dearly and an old teddy she's had since childhood called *'Spot'* that's a Dalmatian. You can find her on the accounts below. Please leave a review of your thoughts on the book and remember to have a creepylicious day...

♥ Instagram: @katyetilstone_author

♥ TikTok: @katyetilstone_author

♥ Facebook: @katyetilstone_author

♥GoodReads: @Katye Tilstone

Candy Cane

Printed in Dunstable, United Kingdom